The Day Before Happiness

The Day Before Happiness

ERRI DE LUCA

Translated by
JILL FOULSTON

ALLEN LANE
an imprint of
PENGUIN BOOKS

ALLEN LANE

UK | USA | Canada | Ireland | Australia
India | New Zealand | South Africa

Penguin Books is part of the Penguin Random House group of companies
whose addresses can be found at global.penguinrandomhouse.com.

First published in Italian as *Il giorno prima della felicità* 2009
First published in this translation by Allen Lane 2016

001

Text copyright © Giangiacomo Feltrinelli Editore Milano, 2009
Translation copyright © Jill Foulston, 2016
All rights reserved

The translator gratefully acknowledges Leonardo Persico for his help with Neapolitan dialect.

Typeset in Dante MT Std by Palimpsest Book Production Ltd, Falkirk, Stirlingshire
Printed in Great Britain by Clays Ltd, St Ives plc

A CIP catalogue record for this book is available from the British Library

ISBN: 978-0-141-39839-6

I discovered the hiding place because the ball ended up there. Behind the niche for the statue in the courtyard was a trapdoor covered by two planks of wood. I noticed them moving when I stepped on them. I got scared, recovered the ball and wriggled out between the legs of the statue.

Only a boy as thin and agile as I was could have slipped his head and body between the barely separated legs of the warrior king. The ball had ended up behind the statue after ricocheting between the sword and one of the legs, and I'd gone round the sword, which was planted just in front of his feet.

I shoved the ball through and the others started playing again while I twisted around to get out. Traps are easy to fall into, but you have to sweat a bit to get out of them. Still, fear spurred me on. I went back to my place in goal. The big boys let me play with them because wherever the ball went, I could get it. It often landed on the first-floor balcony of an abandoned flat. Rumour had it that a ghost lived there. These old buildings were full of walled-up trapdoors, secret passageways, crimes and passions. They were swarming with ghosts.

This is what happened when I climbed on to the balcony for the first time. One afternoon, I was watching the big boys playing football from the little window on the ground floor of the courtyard where I lived. After a bad kick, the ball shot up and landed on the first-floor balcony. It was lost – a Superflex vinyl, a bit deflated from use. While they were bickering over the problem, I leaned out and asked if they'd let me play with them.

Sure, if you buy us another ball. No, with that one, I said. Intrigued, they agreed. I scrambled on to the downpipe running beside the balcony and up to the top. The pipe was thin and fixed to the courtyard wall with rusty clamps. I started climbing. It was covered with dust and my grip wasn't as secure as I'd thought. But I'd committed myself now. I looked up. Behind a window on the third floor was the girl I was hoping to catch sight of. She was in her usual place, her head in her hands. Most of the time she looked up at the sky, but not just then – she was looking down.

I had to keep going – so I kept going. For a kid, five metres is a huge drop. I scaled the pipe, placing my feet on the clamps until I reached the level of the balcony. Below me, the commentary had hushed. I stretched my left hand towards the iron railing; I was a few inches short. So I had to lean out, trusting my feet and still holding on to the pipe. I decided to go for it, and I made it. Now I had to bring my right hand over. I held fast to the iron railing with my left hand and then grabbed it with my right. I lost my footing: for a moment, my hands held my body suspended over the void. I quickly brought my knee up, then two feet, and I clambered over. Why wasn't I afraid? I knew my fear was shy; in order to come out, it had to be alone. But all eyes were on me: those of the boys down below and hers from above. My fear was embarrassed to come out. It would get its own back later – at night, in my bed, when ghosts would rustle through the empty darkness.

I threw the ball down and the boys started playing again without taking any notice of me. Getting down was easier: I could reach for the pipe, counting on two solid supports for my feet on the edge of the balcony. First, though, I quickly glanced at the third floor. I'd volunteered for this feat in the hope that she'd notice me, the little scruff from the courtyard. There she was, staring. But before I could risk a smile, she'd disappeared. How silly of me to check to see if she were watching! I had to believe without seeing, as you do with guardian angels. I got angry with myself and slid down the pipe in order to get off the stage. Below, the prize awaited me: admission to the game. They put me in front of the goal and that was that: my role was decided. I would be goalie.

From that day on, they called me *'a scigna*, a monkey. I'd dive between their feet to grab the ball and save the goal. The goalie is the final defence – he's got to be the last-ditch hero. I took kicks at my hands, in my face, and never cried. I was proud to play with the bigger boys, who were nine, even ten years old.

The other times the ball landed on the balcony, I'd be up there in less than a minute. In front of the defence goal there was a puddle from a leak. At the beginning of the game it was always clear, and I could see the girl at the window reflected there while my team was attacking. I never ran into her, and I didn't know what her body was like under that face in her hands. On sunny days, I managed to get back up to her when the glass bounced her reflection down to my little window, and I'd keep looking at her until the light brought tears to my eyes. The glass panes of the courtyard's closed windows allowed her reflection to show up in my shadowy corner. What a journey her portrait made to reach my little window! A short time before, a television had arrived in one of the apartments in our building. I'd heard that you could see people and animals moving on it, but only in black and white. And yet I could see the girl with all the brown of her hair, the green of her dress, and the sun's yellow glow over everything.

I went to school. My adoptive mother enrolled me, but I never saw her. The porter, Don Gaetano, looked after me. In the

3

evenings, he'd bring me a hot meal, and in the morning before school, I'd take back the clean plate while he warmed me a mug of milk. I lived in a little room, the *stanzino*, by myself. Don Gaetano hardly spoke at all. He'd grown up as an orphan too, but in an orphanage, unlike me. I was free to come and go in our building and around the city.

I liked school. The teacher talked to us children. I came from a little room where no one talked to me, to school, where there was someone to sit and listen to. I took in everything he said. It was a beautiful thing – a man who explained numbers, dates in history and places on the map to children. There was a coloured map of the world, and someone who'd never left the city could recognize Africa, which was green, the South Pole, white, Australia, yellow, and the oceans, blue. Continents and islands were feminine, the seas and mountains masculine.

At school there were the poor kids and the others. Every day at eleven, the caretaker came in with a piece of bread and quince jam for those of us from poor backgrounds, like me, and with him came the mouthwatering scent of the bakery. The others didn't get any; they'd brought snacks from home. Another difference was that in the spring, the poor ones had their heads shaved because of lice; the others got to keep their hair.

We wrote with fountain pens and ink, which sat in a hole in each desk. Writing was like painting. We dipped the pen in the ink, let the droplets fall until just one remained, and managed to write half a word with it. Then we dipped again. We poor ones blew the paper dry, and under our warm breath the blue of the ink trembled as it changed colour. The others dried theirs with blotting paper. Ours was the more beautiful gesture, because it created a breeze over the flat sheet of paper, while the others squashed their words under white card.

★

In the courtyard, the kids played surrounded by the distant past of the centuries. The city was ancient, hollowed out, full of caves and hiding places. On summer afternoons, when the residents were on holiday or had disappeared behind their shutters, I'd go into a second courtyard where the mouth of a cistern was boarded over. I'd sit on it and listen for sounds. From the depths – who knew how far down – came the sound of rippling water. There was life walled up down there: a prisoner, an ogre, a fish. Cool air came up from between the boards, drying my sweat.

I had extraordinary freedom in my childhood. Children are explorers, and they want to discover secrets. So I went back behind the statue to see where the trapdoor led. It was August, the month when kids grow up fastest.

Early one afternoon, I slipped between the feet and the sword of the statue, a copy of the one of Roger, King of Normandy, in front of the Royal Palace. The planks were firmly fixed; they moved, but you couldn't lift them. I'd brought a spoon with me, and I used it to loosen whatever was holding them so tightly. I took off the two planks. Below was darkness, going way down. Fear took hold of me, making the most of the fact that there was no one else around. You couldn't hear any water; the darkness was dry. After a while, though, fear gets bored. The darkness actually seemed less dense, and I could see the rungs of a wooden ladder going down. I stretched out my arm to see if it would hold; it was sturdy, dusty.

I put the planks back over the entrance. I'd discovered enough for one day.

I went back with a candle. A chill came up from the dark and I felt it on my bare legs below my shorts. I climbed down into a cave. The city is hollow underneath, and that's what holds it up. Our mass above is counterbalanced by an equal shadow below. It's this that sustains the body of the city.

When I touched ground, I lit the candle. It was a cigarette-smuggler's stash. I knew there were offshore pickups in motor-boats. I'd discovered a storeroom. I was put out – I'd hoped for some kind of treasure. There had to be another entrance; those crates couldn't have gone through the king's legs. Sure enough, there was a stone staircase opposite the wooden ladder. The big room was quiet; the tufa absorbed the sound. In the corner was a camp-bed, a mattress, some books, a Bible. There was even a toilet, the kind you squat over. I went back up disappointed. I hadn't discovered a thing.

It didn't occur to me to tell the police, nor could it have. To betray a secret, reveal a hideout – a boy doesn't do these things. To children, spying is despicable. It wasn't even that I'd consid-ered the idea and rejected it – it never crossed my mind.

That August I often went down into the storeroom. I liked the coolness and the quiet stillness of the tufa. I'd sit on the rungs of the ladder where the light came in and I started read-ing the books. Not the Bible – God gave me the creeps. That's how I got the reading bug. The first book was *The Three Musket-eers*, though there were four of them. I sat at the top of the lad-der, my feet dangling, my mind lighting up from the books. When I finished those, I wanted more.

Down the alley where I lived were booksellers who sold to students. Second-hand books on offer were kept in wooden boxes on the pavement outside. I started going there, picking out a book and sitting on the ground to read it. One of the booksellers chased me away, so I went to another and he let me stay. He was a good guy, Don Raimondo, the kind of person who understands without explanations. He gave me a stool so I didn't have to sit on the ground to read. Then he said he'd lend me a book if I'd bring it back without ruining it. I thanked him and told him I'd return it the next day. I stayed up all night finishing it. Don Raimondo saw that I was as good as my word and he let me take home a book a day.

I chose the slim ones. It was my summer craze, in the absence of a teacher to tell me new things. They weren't books for children, and there were lots of words in the middle I didn't understand, but the ending, yes, I understood the ending. It was an invitation to escape.

Ten years later, I found out from Don Gaetano that a Jew had hidden in the storeroom during the summer of '43. I was in my last year at school and Don Gaetano was becoming more friendly with me. During the afternoons he taught me to play *scopa*, and how to note the cards taken in a *spariglio* in order to tell which cards were left to play.[1] He always won. He didn't slap the cards down on the table, but he played quickly; I slowed him down while I mentally totted up the cards played. To repay his new trust, I decided to tell him something.

'Don Gaetano, one summer ten years ago I went down into that big room with all the crates.'

'I know.'

'How do you know?'

'I know everything that goes on around here. The dust, *guaglio*'.[2] There were handprints and footprints in the dust on that wooden ladder. You were the only one who could fit between Ruggero's thighs to get down there. They called you a monkey.'

'And you never said anything to me!'

'You didn't say anything either. I kept an eye on you. You went down there, kept your hands off the crates and didn't tell a soul.'

---

1 *scopa*, literally meaning 'broom', is an extremely popular card game in Naples. The *spariglio* is a move in which one card takes two or more which add up to the value of the single card.
2 *guaglio*' is short for *guaglione*, a Neapolitan term for 'boy' or 'kid'.

'I didn't have anyone to tell.'

'What were you doing down there?'

'I liked the dark, and there were books. I picked up the habit of reading down there.'

'A monkey amongst the books. You shinned up the drainpipe quick as a mouse, threw yourself between all those feet to get the ball . . . You had a natural, spontaneous courage.'

'No one told me to do one thing or another. At school I learned what you could and couldn't do. I'm happy to go there, thanks to my adoptive mother. She made me study. This is my last year, and then the scholarship she got me runs out.'

'You're making the most of your studies. You're *roba buona*, good stuff.'

This was his highest compliment – 'good stuff' – a grand title as far as he was concerned.

'But at *scopa* you're a dunce!'

'But tell me, Don Gaetano, what was that ladder doing there behind the statue? Nobody could get down that way.'

'They could: during the war I sawed through one of Ruggero's thighs. You could take it off in an emergency. And, at the time, hiding places were useful – for weapons, black market stuff, anyone who had to hide. Jews were being hunted down and they were worth a lot. Only a few stayed in the city.'

Don Gaetano saw that I was curious to hear stories about what had happened around the time I was born. He made excuses for the people who lived here – war brought out the worst in people – but he had no time for anyone who sold a Jew to the police. Anyone who ratted on them was *''na carogna'*, scum.

'The Jews: were they made of something different from us? So they don't believe in Jesus Christ – neither do I. They are people, like us, born and reared here, and they speak the dialect.

But we had nothing in common with the Germans. They wanted to be in charge, and at the end they put people against the wall, shot them and looted the shops. Yet the moment the city threw itself at them, they ran, just like us. Lost their bravado. What had the Jews done to the Germans? We never did figure it out. Our people barely knew the Jews existed. They were an ancient people. But when it came to making money, everyone knew who was Jewish. If they'd put a price on mythical creatures around here, it would have been possible to find them, even second-hand. Because there were always scumbags who'd give them up.'

Our card games were interrupted by people passing by the lodge, asking questions, leaving or collecting something. Don Gaetano didn't miss a thing. It was an old building with lots of stairways, and he knew everyone's business. Some came to ask his advice. Then Don Gaetano would tell me to watch the lodge and they'd go off. When he came back, he'd pick up the cards and our conversation where we'd left off.

'He was down there until the Americans arrived and up until the last day, he thought I might sell him to the Germans. His own doorman had done it. He just about managed to pull on a pair of trousers and his shirt – no shoes – and escape from the roof. He kept some books packed up and he took those with him. The Jews are brought up to run, just as we're always ready for earthquakes under our feet or the volcano to erupt. The only difference is that we don't leave home with our books.'

'I would, Don Gaetano. I'd take my schoolbooks with me if I had to run from an earthquake.'

'He came to me at night during an air raid. I held the door open and he slipped in. From his breast he'd torn the star they had to sew on, and the threads hung from his lapel. I took him down there, where he stayed for a month, the worst one of the

9

war. When the uprising began, I brought him a pair of shoes I'd taken off a German soldier, and he came out into the liberated city wearing them. He asked me why I hadn't sold him.'

'And how did you answer?'

'What could I say? He'd spent a month underground counting the minutes, wondering if he'd survive or not. Each of his thank-yous was poisoned with suspicion. The war was almost over, and the Americans had arrived in Capri. The thought of being arrested just a few days before liberation really angered him.

'That September was a raging inferno. The Germans were mining the harbour against an American landing. They blew up parts of the city while the blitz continued. The sea suddenly filled up with hundreds of American ships. Fire broke out on all sides. For us, it was about being cheated of our freedom; for him, it was about his life. And it was all hanging on someone who could betray him, or who could be arrested, killed, and not come back to bring him something to eat. When he heard me coming down the stairs, he never knew whether it was me or the end.'

'How did you answer his question about why you didn't betray him?'

'Because I don't sell human flesh. Because war brings out the worst in people, but also the best. Because he came barefoot. Who knows why? I don't remember what I told him. It could be that I didn't answer. At that point the story was finished and the whys didn't matter any more. I heard his thoughts and answered them, but he couldn't hear mine. You can't speak with people's thoughts. They have no voice.'

'Then it's true what they say about you, Don Gaetano? That you hear people's thoughts inside their heads?'

'It's true and it's not. Sometimes yes, sometimes no. And it's better like that, since people have ugly thoughts.'

'If I think something, can you guess what it is?'

'No, *guaglio*'. The thoughts that come to me are the ones that fly through people's heads, the ones a person doesn't even know they've had. If you're minding your own business, it stays with you. But thoughts are like sneezes. They suddenly break out, and I hear them.'

That's how he knew everyone's business. And it's why he had a sort of sadness, as if expecting the worst, but also a half-smile to chase it away. Wrinkles would appear at the corners of his eyes, and the melancholy would drain away.

'Did the Jewish man do a lot of thinking?'

'Yes, he did. When he was reading, no, but the rest of the time, yes – about the Holy Land, about a ship to get there. Europe is lost to us; there's no more life here. He took a belt as an example. He thought, We're the belt around the waist of the world. With our holy book, we're the strip of leather that has held up its trousers ever since Adam realized he was naked. The world has wanted to get rid of that belt many times, to throw it away: it feels too tight. I remember that thought exactly – he entertained it often.

'When he came out into the open, he could barely stand up. He went to his house, but it was occupied. A family had parked themselves there. They'd gone as far as changing the locks. I went to have a word with them and they left, but not before stripping the house. They even took the electrical wires from the walls.'

'How did you persuade them to leave?'

'We all had guns after fighting against the Germans. I went there at night, and I fired through the lock. I went in and told them that I'd come back at noon the next day and I expected to find the house empty. Just like that. He got back into his house, and then sold it a few months later and went abroad, to Israel. He came by the lodge to say goodbye. The city was still in ruins.

"I'm taking a stone from Naples with me. I'll put it in the wall of the house I'm going to have in Israel. We're going to build there with the stones they threw at us.'"

I listened, played *scopa*, lost. In the evenings, I wrote down Don Gaetano's stories. The city itself was my school. I was sorry when summer's lessons were over. The other students were glad, but not me. I consoled myself with the yellowed pages of Don Raimondo's books, which he saved when someone wanted to get rid of them.

'A person spends an entire lifetime filling up their bookshelves, and then their child can't wait to get rid of it all. How do you fill empty shelves – with blocks of cheese? "Just get them out of here," they say. And there goes someone's life: their whims, their investment, their sacrifices, the satisfaction of seeing their knowledge grow by centimetres, like a plant.'

'Don Raimondo, I can't actually repay you for letting me read without charging me anything.'

'It's nothing. You bring them back to me all dusted. When you're a man, you'll come and buy them from me.'

In the summer, the city grew lighter and at night it went out in the streets to breathe. I played *scopa* with Don Gaetano in the courtyard and never won a single game.

'*T'aggia 'mpara' e t'aggia perdere.*' That was his verdict at the end of the game. 'I have to teach you and then I have to let you go.' It was a fact. It had to happen like that. With the city, too, it had to be like that. It had to teach me, then let me go.

At the end of the games I'd go back to my little room to firm up what I'd learned. It was odd, the Jewish man's idea about the belt. I checked mine – it wasn't tight, but I let it out a notch. Even if the world felt the squeeze, it couldn't get rid of the belt. It couldn't go back to before that holy book. I'd read that the world was jealous of the Jews because they were the chosen ones. During the war, they'd been chosen as targets. The man cooped up below the city – even from there he managed to communicate. Why hadn't he taken any books with him when he left the hiding place, or even the Bible?

'I pointed out to him that he was leaving his bundle. He replied that someone else could use it. The Bible too? Then he recited a verse for me that was written in it: "Naked came I out of my mother's womb, and naked shall I return." He was saying that the hiding place had been a place of rebirth for him, and that he had to leave it without any baggage.'

'Don Gaetano, were you hiding a saint?'

'He wasn't a saint. I heard him arguing with God the Father, telling him that his faith was a life-sentence. "We're marked out by circumcision. We wear the charge written on our bodies. Our Father took away his breath and left us mud."

'That was his name for God the Father – "*il nostro*", Our Father. He wasn't a saint, but someone who argued with that Our Father of his.'

'Then you're the saint, the one who risked death in order to hide someone you didn't know.'

'You're looking for a saint in all of this. There aren't any; nor devils either. There are people who do a few good things and a host of bad ones. Any time is good for doing good deeds, but you need an opportunity to do something bad, the right moment. War provides the best chance to do something really nasty. It gives you permission. But you don't need permission to do good.'

A travelling salesman turned up in the courtyard. Don Gaetano looked up, went out and said hello. '*O sapunaro*, the rag-and-bone man, came often, pulling his cart himself. He was wider than he was tall, and each time he came he wasn't satisfied until someone from every apartment had shown their face. His voice would have woken the dead. Don Gaetano nicknamed him 'The Day of Judgement'. He'd take him a bottle of water and the rag-and-bone man would empty it between one shriek and the next.

'Don Gaeta'. Do you remember when we were on the barricades in via Foria?'

It was his calling card. He and two women had overturned a tram in the middle of a thoroughfare to stop the German tanks.

'*Nuie simmo robba bona*. We're made of good stuff.'

Looking at the man's trolley and what people threw out, Don Gaetano understood how the economy worked.

'We're turning into gentlemen: they've thrown out an old bathtub, no less, and they're also throwing away their wool mattresses – they've bought the ones with springs. They're throwing away their treadle sewing machines. They believe in electricity as they do in eternal life. And when it runs out?'

It was an angry summer, almost cold. In July, the summit of the volcano turned white. People played their lotto numbers and they kept coming up. There were some big wins. The year before, a cobbler had chosen four winning numbers.

I asked Don Gaetano if he could tell what numbers people had chosen. He waved at me as if swatting a fly.

But was there an art to it? Could you learn to hear other people's thoughts?

'Well, don't call them people. They're individuals, every one of them. If you call them people, you don't notice each person. You can't hear the thoughts of a people, only those of a person, one at a time.'

It was true. Until that age, I hadn't distinguished individuals. They were all people. That summer, in the lodge, I learned to recognize the tenants. When I was a child, the only one who'd mattered to me was the girl behind the third-floor window. I didn't even know what her parents were like. She'd disappeared, and after that I hadn't bothered getting to know the building's other residents.

'So it's not possible to learn to do what you do, Don Gaetano? Isn't there some kind of art to it?'

'Even if there were, I wouldn't tell you. It's not very nice to know what passes through people's heads. So much spitefulness comes and goes in there without being acted upon. If I said what everyone thought about each other, there'd be civil war.'

'So you hear but you don't get involved?'

'Sometimes I intervene. You've heard about the wins that were breaking the lottery bank with the numbers for snow:[3] one of the tenants in a hovel at the end of the alleyway had chosen well and said nothing to his wife. I called him and said: "You can't do that." He goes, "What?" "You don't just take home your debts. You have to share the good news, too."'

'So what did he do?'

'He went and bought a goat, some wine and showed up with his winnings.'

'But what about hearing a thought you could take advantage of, something you could use personally?'

Don Gaetano gave me a stern look. 'If you find a wallet, do you give it back to the person who lost it?'

'I don't know – it's never happened to me. Without experiencing it, I'd say yes. But I'll only know if it happens to me. I don't know beforehand what I'd do.'

'You're honest. When I find a thought in someone that could be useful to me, I don't pocket it. I leave it there. I can't give it back, saying: "Look, you've lost one of your thoughts!" I act as if I haven't heard it.'

---

3 'numbers for snow' refers to the *smorfia*, a picture book used to choose numbers for the Neapolitan lottery.

'I'd love to know what people are thinking.'

'But if you can't even remember the three unplayed cards from the last hand of *scopa* ... You'll have to learn to play cards first.'

Like me, Don Gaetano was without a family. He'd grown up in an orphanage, and then went to a seminary to train for the priesthood. But they say he fell in love with a prostitute and took off his habit. He went away to Argentina for about twenty years, and came back in 1940 just in time for the war. I knew all this about him before the summer we got close.

'You had a thing for that girl on the third floor. You were always looking up there.'

'I was trying to get her to notice me, the way kids do. But she disappeared all of a sudden. Do you know where she and her family went?'

'I know where she is now. She returned to Naples and she's with a young guy, a *camorrista*. He's in jail. She wasn't for you.'

It all came back to me: my loneliness at that age, the image of myself as a kid, searching for her face behind the window, climbing the stairs in the hope of meeting her ... I put my fingers against the bridge of my nose to catch two tears stealing out. Childhood bonds stick with you.

That night I wrote down Don Gaetano's phrase: you'll have to learn to play cards first. Before what? If I learned how to play *scopa*, would I be able to hear people's thoughts? I couldn't ask. The phrase would have to do.

In the days when Don Gaetano was a child, no one told stories in the orphanages. So he took things into his own hands. He'd make up stories about the lives of animals, kings and vagabonds, and tell them in dialect around the little furnace in the dormitory. The children kept warm and filled themselves up through their ears.

'Neapolitan is made for storytelling. You tell someone some-thing and they believe you. In standard Italian there's always some doubt: did I hear that right? Italian is great for writing, when you don't need a voice, but to tell a story, you want our language, which holds it all together and helps you to see it. Neapolitan invites fantasy. It opens up your eyes and ears. I told the children about life in other places.

'No one ever came to see us, not even on Sundays. If a child grows up without physical affection, his skin toughens up and he doesn't feel anything, even if someone hits him. He has only his ears to teach him about the world. There was plenty of screaming around us, but nobody cried. Children outside the orphanage cried, but nobody inside knew how. Not even when one of us died. It was just normal. The fever would come, blaze up and then die down. We still felt like laughing and play-ing. When it was cold we'd pile up, all hugging each other, becoming one body. We'd change places, and the ones in the outside would trade with the ones in the centre. We made heat, and we made ourselves laugh. If one of us shouted, *'o muntone!*, we'd immediately make a heap, everyone piled up together.

'The big windows at the orphanage looked over the court-yard. The ones facing outside were walled up, since a few of us had jumped out to get away. I was the only person who could scale the gate at night. I was slight, like you, and I went about the city, mingling with the crowds that roam around at night. I'd go to the harbour. I liked the ships. When I was about thirteen, I made friends with a prostitute my age. I'd do things for her, and warn her if the police were around. When she was finished, and I had to go back to the orphanage, she'd pay me with a glass of milk and a brioche. We were alike, a brother and a sister who'd get together sometimes. But then she found someone to marry and she left for the north.

'The city is beautiful at night. There's danger, but there's also freedom. Insomniacs: artists, murderers, hustlers all roaming around. The taverns are open, the fried-food kiosks, the cafés. We greet one another, we get to know each other, us night-owls. Everyone excuses their own vices. Daylight accuses us; the dark of night gives absolution. The transvestites come out, men dressed like women because nature tells them to be like that, and no one hassles them. At night, no one asks for explanations. Cripples, the blind, the lame, they all come out, people who are spurned by day. Night in the city is like a pocket turned inside out. Even the homeless dogs come out. They wait for night so they can look for scraps. Lots of them get by on their own. By night, the city is a civilized place.

'I had restless legs. I ran all over, found things to eat. They say it's their legs, not their teeth, that allow wolves to eat. During the day, I used that energy to tell the children stories. No one in there had a name, so we made them up. One was called Bite, because he had no teeth. We named the lame one The Train for Foggia, because he was always late. Another one was Sleep, since he was always half asleep; yet another one was Whistle, because he whistled like a pedlar. As the oldest of us, I was Grandpa. Many of them had never glimpsed the sea, so I told them about it: it was a seesaw of water, and boats played on it, passing from one wave to another. I showed them what a wave was with a sheet.

For those of us inside, the way to get an education was the seminary. So I went to one. And from there too I escaped at night.'

On summer evenings, people walked the streets to get a bit of air near the shore. It wasn't the nocturnal city Don Gaetano had known – that one got going later – after the evening stroll. To refresh ourselves after a game of *scopa*, the two of us in the courtyard would sit still and quiet, or sometimes he would talk. For the sake of contrast, he'd cast his mind back to the violent summer of '43. Out in the open, he had to lower his voice so it wouldn't echo round the courtyard.

'Before I saw him standing outside, barefoot, with books tucked under his arm, I'd never thought about hiding anyone. I kept a bit of black market stuff down there and towards the end, a few guns taken from the police. But when I saw him there at the door, I pulled him inside. I'd go to visit him during the air raids, when the *palazzo* emptied out as people ran for the shelters. I stayed to guard the place, since during the bombing, maurauders would go round robbing houses. They were afraid of nothing, and how those bombs fell all over the city! I'd visit him during the alerts, so that he could talk a little. Down there, the war was muffled, the bombs just someone knocking at the door. The tufa absorbed the din, took the impact without shaking. The bombs came crashing down but they didn't shake the walls. Tufa is a bomb-shelter.'

'What did you talk about down there?'

'We played *scopa*. I taught him how and he picked it up immediately. He didn't want to lose. He was different from you. It doesn't matter to you. I liked his stubbornness. This guy, who'd lost everything, who put his life in the hands of a stranger, insisted on not losing at *scopa*. He was someone who took everything seriously.

'"You're too serious for a Neapolitan," I told him. But he answered, "Not at all! I'm laughing away down here. Outside there's war, the slaughter of my people, the fall of the city I was born in, and here I am, as if I were standing in a doorway waiting for a squall to pass. And here you are, too, coming to entertain me. I read the holy book and our prophets and I start laughing. Down here, the year of grace 1943 for you and our year 5704, it's an amusing read. I'm not serious, Don Gaetano, I'm tragic, a reject from the comic sort. Let me at least take the game of *scopa* seriously – it's almost a sacred art! I mean it: sacred. The most important card is number 7, and that's a special number for us Jews. It was the Jews who invented the week. Before that, calendars went by the sun and moon. Then our god let us know that there were six days plus one. We were the ones to sanctify the number 7, before *scopa*. There are forty cards in a deck, just like the number of years we were in the desert, between the exodus and entering the Promised Land. Then there's the *spariglio*, a variation on taking one card with another of equal value, which lets you take several cards that add up to the number on that single card. This is an invention you don't find in nature. Nature is for couples; *scopa* is for breaking them up. The dealer wants to keep everything paired up, his opponent, no. It's a battle between order and chaos. So let me take the game of *scopa* seriously."'

'When he spoke to me like that, I got the shivers and kept quiet.'

'I've got them too, listening to you remembering what he said. I have to write it down the same day in order not to forget it, but you can remember it almost twenty years later.'

'It's all to do with the game. If you can remember the cards that were picked up, you can do the same with thoughts.'

'I'd come up dazed from those visits. Up here, it was September of '43 and down below, it was a month in 5704 of the Hebrew calendar. Down there was a man from ancient times, a contemporary of Moses and the Pharaohs, who happened to live at the same time as the Nazis. It was a good thing I couldn't hear him laughing below. "Don Gaetano, let me know when you see stars in the middle of the day."

'Outside, the kids stole guns from the barracks and hid them. One group with a guy dressed like a *carabiniere* had emptied the armoury at the fortress of St Elmo. Meanwhile, the Germans were ransacking the churches. They blew up the San Rocco bridge at Capodimonte, and we saved the one at Sanità by removing the explosives. We did the same with the aqueduct. They wanted to leave the city in ruins. The uprising was our salvation.

'Along with the good came the bad. A decent person took to lending at high interest, a young girl from a good family prostituted herself to the Germans. The guy who was known as *guappo*, a thug, was the first to run for the shelter. The Germans and the Fascists got worse, because the war was going badly. The landing at Salerno had succeeded. They blew up the factories and plundered the warehouses, leaving them empty. During those last days of September, the hunger and exhaustion in people's faces made the city a dreadful place to be. If you had anything, you ate it in hiding. The Germans set things up. They'd force open a shop and invite people to raid it. They'd fire into the air while the crowd threw themselves on the stuff, and then they'd film the scene as propaganda: a German soldier intervenes to stop looting. This is the sort of thing that could happen, *guaglio'*, on any given day during that beautiful September.'

Sitting on two chairs in the courtyard, we looked up to where the city ended and who-knows-what began, perhaps the universe. It was close, a piazza ringed round by a fence. Don Gaetano gazed at it, his hands folded, and sighed. I bent my neck back too: that field above and beyond the balconies moved in a circle, very slowly, but it made your head spin all the same. Your eyes, which normally couldn't see beyond the horizon, managed to see the planets. No wonder the sky went to your head and made you believe you could go there.

'They bombed every night. The city was constantly running, not even shouting, just running and saving its breath. The German bombings were mixed up with the American raids. The siren would sound only after the flak had started up.'

Then he'd remember something curious and start smiling. 'A young lad was walking around arm in arm with his girl when the siren sounded. He couldn't run off by himself, and she couldn't run in her heels. So you saw him pulling her along and she came lurching behind him, shrieking, "Leave me! Leave me!" but he wouldn't – he had to drag her by force.

'The girls were more courageous, but the young men redeemed themselves during those days in late September. Men need special circumstances to draw out their courage. Women are braver during normal times – if you could call '43 normal.'

'People emerged from the shelters after the air raids to find their houses gone. The faces of those who'd lost everything between one hour and the next: an old man was sitting on the rubble of his *palazzo*, gazing up into the sky. He came over to me and said, "*Sto guardanno 'ncielo*. I'm looking up to the heavens to see where I can settle. Because down here on earth, I've got nothing left anymore." People searched through collapsed houses for something to save. They rummaged around, going through doors from one room to another, even though the walls were no longer there. They'd go into the kitchen to see if they'd turned off the gas, and then they'd look up and see sky instead of a ceiling. That arrogant sky of September '43, a tablecloth with embroidered edges, fresh and clean, without a speck of dust, spotless. A still, deep blue: Come down to earth for a while, sky . . . let's trade places. Take the stench up there, and spread your cloth down here on earth. A spiteful sky, miles away, not starting from your terrace like it does these days.

'As the rain came, so the revolt began. It was as if the city had been waiting for an agreed sign, that the sky had clouded over. And the Americans stopped their bombing.'

'The Jew used to ask me what the weather was doing. I told him it wasn't doing anything, nothing was changing, and it wasn't letting a drop of rain fall on the dust. There was no water, and the women had to go and get it in buckets from the sea or they couldn't do their laundry. All that lovely, stable weather bothered the Jew too. He asked me if you could see any stars by day. He was waiting for a sign. "Most people like sunny days, but they scare me. The worst things happen under a blue sky. When the weather's bad, people postpone their misdeeds. But when the sun shines, anything goes. If I make it through to the autumn, I hope to dance under a downpour."

'"By autumn the war will be over. The Americans are in Salerno." I didn't tell him that you could already see them – he would have gone crazy to get out of there. I heard his thoughts: So close to freedom and I can't see it. Shut up down here wondering if this will turn out to be a trap instead of my salvation! They'll open the door and come down to get me. He didn't want to allow the thought that I might betray him to enter his head. If not me, then someone from the *palazzo* who had found out. He asked me if anyone else knew about the hiding place. My reassurance wasn't enough.

'"This is no time to trust anyone, and I'm not asking you to trust me. But don't give in to negative thinking. Don't leave here looking for a safe place – there aren't any. If you go out, they'll shoot you on the spot. Commander Scholl issued an order for all men aged between eighteen and thirty-three to report to the barracks or be shot. Of the 30,000 they were expecting, only 120 showed up."

'Have you grasped what the war was like, *guaglio*'? There were more deaths among civilians than soldiers. I started hearing thoughts in the streets: Why are they staying in the city and not going off to fight? Why are they lording it over us poor people instead of going to the front? The thoughts began in just one head. But when individuals form a crowd, it amounts to something.

'So one morning comes, a Sunday at the end of September, and finally it rains and I hear the same word in everyone's mouth, spat out from the same thought: *mo' basta*, enough's enough. It was a wind, and it wasn't coming from the sea, but from inside the city: *mo' basta, mo' basta*. If I closed my ears, I could hear it louder. The city was sticking its head out of the bag. *Mo' basta, mo' basta*, a drum roll called, and young kids came out with their guns. The uprising centred around the Liceo Sannazaro. The students were the first. Then the men hidden underneath the city came out. They came up from under the ground, as if at a resurrection. "Get 'em! Give it to 'em!" The roads were blocked by barricades. In Vomero they were digging up plane trees and using them to block the tanks. We put about thirty trams together to form a barricade in via Foria. The city sprang like a trap. Four days and three nights. It was like it is now, the end of September.'

'The tanks managed to get by the barricade in via Foria, heading for via Roma. They got down to Piazza Dante, and there they were stopped. Giuseppe Capano, fifteen years old, slipped between the treads of a tank, set off a hand grenade and got out from under it before it exploded. Assunta Amitrano, aged forty-seven, took a slab of marble from her dressing table, threw it from the fourth floor on to a tank and wrecked its machine gun. Luigi Mottola, a fifty-one-year-old who worked in the sewers, sprang up from a manhole under the belly of one of the tanks and blew it up with a gas cylinder. A seventeen-year-old student at the conservatory, Ruggero Semeraro, opened the doors on to the balcony and started playing *The Marseillaise* on the piano, music that makes you feel even more courageous. At the barricade in front of the Bank of Naples, Antonio La Spina, a sixty-seven-year-old priest, shouted out Psalm 94, the one about revenge. The barber, Santo Scapece, thirty-seven, poured a basin of foam over the window of a tank, and it crashed into the metal shutter of a florist's. In the space of three days, we citizens perfected our aim. Bottle bombs ruined tanks and set them on fire. I became a pro at making them, and I'd put a few soap flakes inside the bottles because they ignite better that way. The fishermen from Mergellina gave us the diesel. They couldn't put out to sea because of the mines and the military blockade.

'Six individuals in the thick of a ready crowd made the right moves to foil an armoured attack by the most powerful army, which had already conquered half of Europe on its own. It wasn't the first time six individuals had accomplished such a deed. Long before this, in 1799, the French army, the most powerful of the time, was stopped at the entrance to the city by an uprising of the people after the Bourbon army had melted away.

'Six individuals with names, surnames, ages and occupations kept the Germans from recapturing this city. Six individuals chosen by chance and necessity managed to sort out the situation, while all around them the others, however well intentioned, were missing the mark. When six individuals rise up all at once, that's when you win.'

'And where is that people now, Don Gaetano?'

'In its own place. It hasn't moved and it hasn't been forgotten. When a people comes together and makes its move, it breaks up just as suddenly, and goes back to being a crowd of individuals. They go about doing their own things, but more light-heartedly, because an uprising cheers the people who take part in it.

'The skirmishes of the third day were more intense. We had to drive out the Fascists, who were shooting at us from the roofs. During those battles I managed to get to the hiding place to take the Jew something to eat. The third day I went down to him at dawn and told him that if I didn't come back within twenty-four hours, he could come out. That day, he asked me to do him a favour.

'"Go down to the shore and throw a stone in the water for me." I thought he'd gone a bit mental from being down there. I told him I didn't know if I could go to the shore, since the city was in revolt. "It's one of our rituals, and tomorrow is our New Year. We celebrate it in September. When we throw the stone into the water, we're doing it to relieve ourselves of our sins. For us, the year begins tomorrow. Our god wants today to be the day before happiness."

'He hadn't gone soft in the head. So before seeing the leader of the uprising for my orders, I went to Santa Lucia, where the women were going to get water. I climbed on a rock and threw a really heavy stone into the sea. It was New Year's Day for the Jews and so it had to be for us, too. That day, the city let off its best fireworks – explosions of freedom. The Germans were retreating, pursued and shot at from every rooftop and street corner. They fired the last cannons at Capodimonte. One fell in front of our *palazzo* door and exploded at its base. In his hiding place, the Jew was thrown from his camp-bed and he hit his head. He tore his shirt into shreds and bandaged it. I found him like that in the evening when I took him the news that the Germans had gone.'

'"Have you won?" He didn't believe me.

'"You've won, too."

'"It's the first victory since the time of Judas Maccabeus. And our city, too, it's the first time we've won a war."

'"It's also the first time you've hit your head falling out of bed."

'He asked me if I'd thrown the stone in the sea. "Yes," I answered, "so it's New Year for the city, too." I tended his wound, cleaning the cut with a bottle of brandy I had on me for celebrating the war's end. We drank a couple of glasses. It made us giddy. I had to crawl back upstairs.

'The next day, the city was free. The Germans tried to come back, but we blocked them and they gave up. The Jew came out, leaning on me, eyes closed. With the bandage around his head, he looked like someone coming up out of another world. The city was destroyed. We went to the shore, where the American warships were so many grey rocks sticking up in the middle of the bay. He leaned on me, his feet in a pair of German shoes slapping on the ground. "I don't want to walk on tiptoe anymore." The first Jeeps with a star painted on their hoods passed us in via Caracciolo. "The stars went to war, as it is written in the Song of Deborah. And here are stars in broad daylight."

'"Open your eyes now, just a little. Take a peek."

'He put his hand to his forehead and watched as freedom arrived.

'"You're free," I said, and we embraced one another. Everyone was embracing. We almost missed out on the day before happiness.'

While Don Gaetano was speaking, I looked up at the third-floor window. The day before happiness had not yet come for me. I wanted to know when it was coming, since I didn't want it to happen all of a sudden without my knowing it the day before. The Jews knew it had to happen the day after.

I spent the rest of the night in my room, writing down Don Gaetano's story.

In summer I wake up early and go to the rocks at Santa Lucia with my net to find sea urchins, and maybe even an octopus. I stay there for a couple of hours, before the sun comes up over the shoulder of the volcano. Then gentlemen heading home from late-night parties start spilling out of the clubs. As the first light of day catches them in their evening dress, they hurry to get back indoors, along with the last of the bats. I see the count coming out, too, the one who lives in our *palazzo* and stakes his property at the clubs' tables. He doesn't see me. Gentlemen have a different perspective from ours. We have to look at everything, but they see only what they want to see.

I roll my trousers up to the knee and climb down the rocks. I dunk my net and pull it up, dragging it against the rock face. Through some stroke of luck, I've found something to bring to the table. Before going home, I stop by Don Raimondo's to return a book. He lets me take another, chosen by him. Don Raimondo is an adventurous bookseller, rescuing libraries even from rubbish bins. More often, he's called to a house in mourning, where they're clearing out the deceased's belongings.

'Books retain someone's imprint even more than their clothes or shoes. Heirs get rid of them as a kind of exorcism, a way of banishing the ghost, with the excuse that they need the space, they're being suffocated by all the books. But what do you put in their place, against walls that still bear the trace of their outlines?'

Don Raimondo says to me what he can't say to them. 'The emptiness you feel before a bare wall after its collection of books has been sold off is the most profound one I know. I take those banished books away and give them a second life. Like the second coat of paint that adds the finishing touch, a book's second life is its best.' He salvaged the books of someone who'd been passionate about American literature, and I'm reading the great adventures of that place where so many Neapolitans have gone to live. But it's obvious that they don't write books.

American writers have names all their own. Theirs is a sporting approach to life: a person has to make his own way. It seems like nobody has a family; the one relationship is marriage. Or maybe their books are written by orphans.

One afternoon, Don Gaetano and I went to see a wartime bomb defused. Quite a few fell without exploding. The workmen found one in the harbour when they were digging out a new dock. You couldn't go down there, but Don Gaetano knows all the alleyways and we looked on from a good viewpoint. Meanwhile he continued with his stories about the days of liberation.

'The Fascists had disappeared. You couldn't see any black shirts in the streets. They'd all been dyed grey, the colour *nuncepenzammocchiù* – we're not going to think about that anymore. Around here, we tend to forget the bad as soon as a bit of good comes our way – and that's how it should be. A big round of applause for the Americans, and we just get on with things. But they should have applauded us, since we cleared the way for them.

'I started digging up bombs with them. I brought you to see this because this was my work. There were plenty of them, buried all over the place. One in ten failed to detonate on impact. I even took them from the cemetery. We'd dig around them, then the bomb-disposal expert would arrive to defuse it or, if worst came to worst, explode it. I did that job for a year. It paid well. We workers called them "eggs", left by the war to hatch.

'Some of them exploded while we were shifting the debris. A worker hit something with his pickaxe and a stray stone set off the fuse. So the war continued with these "eggs" that kept on hatching afterwards. You couldn't even find a finger. The blast killed the guy next to you as well. It burst your internal organs. Everything seemed OK on the outside, but everything was ruptured inside. I'm telling you these things so that if you become president one day and they want you to declare war, you'll be twisting the top off your pen ready to put your name on the page – and all at once you'll remember this stuff and – who knows? – you might say, "I'm not signing."'

'President? Me? I can't string two words together.'

'And why not you? You know how to sit and listen. If you're going to be a talker, you have to be a good listener.'

'Don Gaetano, you're confusing me. I'll never be in charge of anyone. But I won't forget what you've said. Weren't you afraid of working with bombs?'

'I wouldn't do it now. At the time, you felt you had to lend a hand to clear away the destruction. The work suited me: I didn't have anyone. No one would have mourned me. The thought makes you feel lighter. Beside me were fathers of families who had to earn their living with trembling knees. They implored the saints with every stroke of the axe. Some of them were doing the work because valuables could be found under the rubble. When something valuable was uncovered, you were meant to shout out and hand it over to the foreman. The rule of war said that anyone who profited would get into serious trouble. But all the same, some of them risked it and hid stuff.'

From our spot on the rocks you could see the fuse of a bomb. Someone in uniform was bustling about.

'He's deactivating it. You can see that the fuses are in good nick, not rusted. If you unscrew them, there's a risk of sparks. Once, a bomb fell right down a lift shaft. It wasn't possible to demolish the walls around it – someone had to go down from above and defuse it. The American bomb-disposal expert wouldn't touch it. I knew the ropes, so I came forward. "I'll go if you give me what he gets." They lowered me on a rope and I unscrewed it and took it out. It was as silent down there as it was in the hiding place. It was winter, but it was warm in there. I was stuck between the bomb and the lift cables, but I was comfortable. They'd cleared the building and were waiting for me. I rested. It was better for me to take my time so the job would seem like it was more difficult. I fell asleep and didn't know where I was when I woke up. Two hours had gone by. I pulled on the rope and they hauled me up, very slowly, since I was holding the fuse in my arms.'

In front of us, the bomb-disposal expert moved back and forth along the crest of the bomb. I saw Ahab on Moby Dick.

'Don't think negatively,' said Don Gaetano, who'd heard my thoughts. 'He's got it.' We saw the man get up and go off with something in his arms. We went home. It was a Sunday afternoon in September, and the crowds were coming down to the shore to get some fresh air. We went up our alleyway, turning to look at the city before going into it. An American aircraft carrier was anchored in the middle of the bay, and around it a hundred little sailboats raced each other between the buoys. All of them crowded together, in a small area, surrounded by the vastness of the sea.

There were plenty of Don Gaetano's stories, too, and all of them contained in just one person. He would say it was because he'd lived at a low level, and stories are water that collects at the bottom of a slope. A man is a basin for collecting stories: the lower he is, the more he receives.

In our building they started asking Don Gaetano: 'Have you got yourself an assistant?' I handed out the post, taking his place when he was called to someone's apartment.

Don Gaetano could fix anything. He had a sure hand and he knew just what to do. Trouble disappeared under his fingers. It was quite something to witness it. Even if he didn't have the right materials or the tool he needed, he sorted it out.

'Don Gaeta', there's a draught coming in under the window and it's making my back hurt near my kidneys – it's that what-d'you-call-it, *areonautic*[4] pain – and that guy, the carpenter won't come.'

The response was like first aid.

'Don't let it get you down! There's a remedy for everything. If there weren't, what would we do when the tissue-maker died, stop blowing our noses? I'll be right up.'

There was a ruder version: The slops man has died, so no more shitting! Don Gaetano preferred the one about tissues. He took some newspaper, wet it and shoved it into the spot where the draught was coming in. It was better than plaster.

I studied at night. School was easy for me. I understood the lessons. They were boxes: what I put into them, I got out of them.

I was seventeen and didn't know a single girl. I kept thinking about the one on the third floor, who all this time had been growing up inside me. I looked at girls in the street, searching for one who could be her. She'd multiplied into various possibilities. She was the one for me, but destiny is not a certainty and you can get separated from it. Destiny is an elusive thing. One day I looked up at the third floor and she wasn't there anymore. I felt a silence throughout my entire body. I spoke quietly, breathed quietly, went around on tiptoe. Seeing those closed shutters made me want to stop making noise. I even stopped my exploring, my searches for hidden treasure. It's obvious that the third-floor window had spurred me on in my adventures.

4 She means rheumatic.

'You should have been born in the Middle Ages, during the time of the knights errant,' said Don Gaetano. He'd heard my thoughts.

But this is the Middle Ages too, I replied mentally. The city contains all eras. Our building and its residents are the Middle Ages in modern dress. In this city, they still vote for the king – not for the King of Savoy, but for Roger of Normandy.[5]

There were regular interruptions to our afternoon games. The widow on the second floor used to call on Don Gaetano. Stuff was always breaking in her house. Don Gaetano left the deliveries to me while he went up with his toolbox. She was a beautiful woman, dark as blackberries in September. She wore strict mourning and spoke in a hoarse voice from behind a black veil. Another regular interruption was the count, who was always staking his property at the club. He had only one apartment left, the one he lived in. His wife, a fine seamstress, made clothes at home, while he went out to play. He'd never worked a day in his life.

'Never, Don Gaetano, never has anyone of my lineage worked. So should I be the one to dishonour the family?'

'I should hope not!' Don Gaetano returned.

'And does this kid know how to play?' he asked.

'No, he's a dunce.'

'Too bad. But you are the champion! I don't know anyone who could equal you. Won't you do me the honour of pairing up with me at *scopone*? We'd break the bank at the club, the two of us together.'

It was pointless, but the count insisted.

'I'll cover any losses and we'll divide the winnings. Together

5 Roger II, a Norman king of Sicily, ruled Naples in the first half of the twelfth century.

we'd make a killing at the club. Do me the honour – and allow me the satisfaction.'

Don Gaetano held out, saying he couldn't enter a gentlemen's club. To make amends, he'd invite the count to come and play with him in the lodge. He knew it was impossible. The count, accustomed to this answer, gave up and said goodbye, trailing behind him a whiff of aftershave, which stung your nose. Don Gaetano said the club was the realm of cheats, where fools like the count got robbed without even noticing it. 'They can steal your socks without even taking off your shoes.'

Don Gaetano missed nature as he'd known it in Argentina. On the plains where herds grazed freely, lightning struck 'to the rhythm of the *tarantella*, and the earth was the sky's dance floor'. 'It was normal to be an orphan there. Everyone was, animals and men alike on plains as vast as the ocean. Thieves, defrocked priests, anarchists, the Irish . . . Argentina lifted the weight off your heart and gave you back all the space you could ever want. The solitude evoked by its vast horizons gave your breathing a new rhythm. I went there not even knowing how to start a fire, and Argentina taught me how to get by, what it is to live from day to day. It's different from existing, which is just passing time. When you're getting by, you only think about the end of the day, a good place to bed down, water for the horses and twigs for a fire.

'I was in Buenos Aires at first. I taught Latin to the children of rich immigrants. Then I went off with an Irishman who was planning to raise sheep on the plains. After a while, I left him too and lived as the guest of nature and its bounty. I had one life, the number assigned to everyone without guarantee. I could have gone down to zero at any moment; I had to earn my time.

'I got to know what fire is on the plains of Argentina. I saw it ignited by bolts of lightning, watched it hide and sneak under torrents of rain, when it would dart lizard-like under the flattened grass and stick out its head. Then the wind would roll it into a ball, and it would leap up on to a bush and dance atop it. I've seen it follow beasts, snatch birds from the air. I've watched it go on the attack, its orange spine climbing up a hill, a trombone of black smoke running ahead of it.'

When he spoke about Argentina, Don Gaetano used another language and a second, throatier voice. His words fell out of him rough, nervous, in need of reining in.

'I stuck close to the fires for the good hunting, but more because they lured me. The air was acrid and my eyelashes got singed. The horse sneezed in fear, but it was proud and put up with it. Fire leaves the earth black and white, sucks the marrow out of all the colours, strips away the green, blue and brown. At night I'd set up camp some way away; the fire I lit would scent the blazes and call out to join them. At dawn I'd smother it, stomping it down to the last cinder. And the fire hated me, because I was in charge and it couldn't bear it. Fire is skilled at surrounding you, suddenly springing up from the other side and advancing even against a wind. It snarls when surrounded.'

All these memories gave Don Gaetano a faraway look. 'I knew nothing about fire. I was born when the volcano was shooting up towards the heavens rather than emptying itself on earth. You'd sweep sacks of ashes from the roofs. That's how I found out that ash isn't light, and that if it builds up, your ceiling will collapse. I saw fire again later in Naples. The bombs started it, and it fell like lightning from on high, but it burned people and houses instead of prairies.

'I didn't recognize it. It resembled men: isolated, and going from one house to the next only rarely. I saw it lash out, extinguish itself, and leave walls standing, even books, with their covers singed and only the title missing. A book is a sea anemone: if it stays tightly closed, it can withstand fire. The air-raid fires were man made, one of our imitations. I'd sit still watching them, wouldn't move a muscle to put them out. Beware of fire, *guaglio'*, because it calls to you, draws you close in wonderment, and makes a fool of you.

'Here, we're nothing, all piled on top of each other in these alleys. There, if I met someone, he was either a blood brother or a murderer. Argentina was a country of refugees. Those who'd fled there stopped looking back.

'I travelled on horseback, with butterflies for company. Millions of them fly low over the surface of the earth, making us run over their shadows. Their shadowy carpet hovers round the horse's hooves. I rode over a flying prairie. At night, if I couldn't find a tree or a rock, I'd tie the horse to my leg, and I'd wake up somewhere else, having been dragged there by the horse as it moved around looking for grass.

'In Argentina, I forgot. Every new thing I learned erased something from my previous life. I began hearing people's thoughts. At first, I took them for voices, and thought maybe I'd gone a bit mental with all that solitude. Then I realized they were other people's thoughts. I couldn't do anything to keep them out. Knowing other people's thoughts is like standing in a porter's lodge. You've got the keys to the houses in your pocket. You're the custodian. You know their sadness, their troubles, their crimes. You're not their confessor, and you can't absolve them. Humanity from the inside is terrifying; meat for roasting in hell. You have to act like you don't know. It was nature, in Argentina, that made me the way I am, that gave me my freedom. A man needs nature, and you haven't experienced it.'

I knew nothing about nature or the body. I'd grown up skinny and hungry, and my only outlet was football on Saturday afternoon, with a training session in the middle of the week. The rocks at Santa Lucia were the sea. Nature was whatever ended up in my net.

Sometimes I'd see the bay from a bend in the road on the hill. All that beauty, invisible to someone who lived inside the city, seemed impossible. We were fish in the net, and all around us was the wide open sea. From up on the hill, I'd look for our alley, but I couldn't find it – the streets were packed like sausages. We lived down there with no idea of how different the light and the air were just a metre above the city. From the curve on the hill, nature made a semi-circle of earth, with Vesuvius at its centre. Nature existed, if you saw it from afar.

One Sunday, Don Gaetano took me up the volcano.

'You should get to know him. He's the head of the house, and we're his tenants. Anyone born here owes him a visit.'

We climbed up through the broom, then over scree. We came to the edge of the crater, a lake-sized hole, where the drizzle vanished before reaching the ground. The summer cloud soaked us, drenched as we were in sweat and rain. There was peace in that blanket of mist, a tense peace that concentrated your blood. Standing at the edge of the volcano after our climb, I noticed that I had an erection. I moved away from Don Gaetano and told him I had to answer the call of nature. A few steps down into the crater, I slipped into the thick of the cloud and tossed off, spraying the compacted ash.

Don Gaetano called out for me and I found him.

'This is nature, *guaglio'*. When you find yourself alone in some god-forsaken place and know who you are.'

I was dazed. The cloud had invited me into her bath, breathed her vapour in my face and kept me inside her. Whether my eyes were open or shut, I saw the same thing: a veil over my eyelids and white blood rising to the end of my prick. It was nature, and I was experiencing it for the first time. I already knew what it was to wake up wet, but the touching and the thrusting inside the cloud had been my own doing. On our descent, we suddenly came into the sun, and it dried our clothes.

I brought home some fish to eat which I'd swept up in my net. Don Gaetano appreciated it and knew how to cook it. He teased me: 'We're eating the unlucky fish again today, the ones who've had the misfortune to go for a *passeggiata* at the same time as you.'

He thought I needed to experience the sea. He knew a fisherman from Mergellina who'd moved to Ischia, and he arranged for me to go out with him.

I caught the last ferry of the day. Emigrants were leaving from the next dock, while I was just going on a jaunt. I felt a bit lost, and I kept my hands in my lap, not sure what else to do with them. The crossing confused my senses: the funnel blowing black as squid's ink against the setting sun, the motor's vibration tickling my skin and the bites I took from a fried ricotta pizza unyoked me from the city for the first time. My eyes said goodbye as the distance grew between us. That two-hour crossing was a kind of farewell, and I wasn't sure whether it was happy or sad.

I landed on the island in the evening. A short stocky man wearing a beret was waiting for me at the dock. He made me laugh when he said, 'You're so tall and thin! Side by side we're like a bomb and a fuse.'

We went to the shore, pushed his boat into the water and rowed out to sea. It was a night that opened up your pores, and no matter where I looked, I was astonished. There was no moon; you had to make do with the stars to see far away. The lights of the island disappeared behind us. Before us and over-head, the sky was brimming with galaxies. From the *palazzo* courtyard it wasn't possible to see how many there were. At school, the universe we studied was a table arranged for guests with a telescope. But here it was, spread out before my naked eyes, looking like a mimosa in March, dangling with clusters of blossom and weighted with a confusion of flowers scattered willy-nilly through the branches so that they hid the trunk.

They fell right down to the edge of the boat. I saw them between the oars and above the beret on his head. That man, the fisherman, didn't notice a thing. Is it really possible for someone to get used to such a sight? To be surrounded by all those stars and not even feel like shaking them off? Thank you, thank you, thank you, my eyes said, for being there.

Out on the open sea, he said, 'You have a go,' and he gave me the oars. Long strokes, pushing on them standing up, fac-ing the prow. He told me to head for a promontory. He set to, baiting a long wire from which lines and hooks dangled every few metres.

I'd seen how it was done with the oars, and I did the same. It wasn't about straining your arms. You had to bend your entire frame forwards and then backwards, lifting the oars and plung-ing them back in. If the waves weren't choppy, the boat slid along by itself under your feet. When that happens, it seems like the sea is dropping. 'Go slowly,' he said 'don't tire yourself out.'

For two hours I rowed through the still waters of the night. The oars made the sound of two syllables, the first one accented when they met the water and a second, longer syllable when they came out. *An*-na, *An*-na . . . With a breath between them, the two syllables formed the name of a woman. After two hours he took the oars and I slowly let the wire with a hundred baits down into the sea. When we had finished, the day was just beginning.

A shiver passed across the surface of the water all around us. Anchovies menaced by a tuna bubbled up in a ball, sending ripples across the water in their flight. We were right in the middle of it. The fisherman grabbed the net and randomly sank it into the middle of the swarm. He pulled out a handful of them live, and threw them into a pail. It was stealing.

The sun came creeping out . . . the sound of gas flaming up . . . the little burner lit . . . and on it, he put a coffee pot all dented and discoloured. He splashed his head and put his beret back on; I did the same. The coffee pot whistled through its beak like a rooster. He lifted his cup towards the sun to greet the coming day. We drank, drawing the scent of the earth through our noses in the middle of the sea, a mile from shore.

At a sign from him, I headed for the sandbank, a field in the midst of the sea that could be found if you looked for a few things: the entire outline of the Sant'Angelo promontory would appear and then the island of Vivara would show up as a bay leaf. In those waters, we rested on the sandbank. The sun was already so bright it brought perspiration to your face. Give us this day our *pane azzurro*, dangling from the hook . . . His slow movements were a prayer, rather than a demand. And approached in this way the sea let us gather. We let down lines baited with small pieces of squid. The first to come up from the deeps was the shimmering white of the croaker fish, then the angry red scorpion fish. Under the sun the sea started to heave, slow waves moving the boat away from the spot. I used the oars to correct the drift. We were waiting to pull up the net, left between two floats.

We went to get them. He slowly pulled the line back into

the baskets, his arms moving rhythmically. We'd gone about fifty metres when a moray eel starting jumping along beside us. He scooped it up with a net, took the bait it had swallowed from its mouth and threw it into a tub. A small grouper followed, then a medium one, and a glorious *sarago*, pin-fish, the fisherman's trophy.

A couple of times my line went tight, stuck somewhere on the sea-bed. He got me to row in one direction, guessing from which side it could be freed. We stopped and took turns at the oars. We went with the current, every stroke pushing the poop forward. We got back to the beach we'd set off from as the bell sounded for midday mass. He offered me the small grouper and shook my hand, which was bleeding because I wasn't used to rowing. We'd maybe exchanged ten words, at the right moments.

On the ferry going home, I stretched out to sleep on seats smelling of varnish and salt. A sailor woke me up when we arrived. The city was all around us and I hadn't sensed it coming closer. I was confused for a bit, and didn't know where to turn or what to do. The stinging in my hands got me going.

That evening Don Gaetano cooked the best grouper in the world with tomatoes, and we stripped it clean off the bone.

It was summer, and I often felt that swelling in my trousers. Don Gaetano taught me a few simple plumbing and electrical jobs so he could send me to do some of the repairs instead of him. I got a few tips.

One afternoon, when the widow called as usual, he told me to go. I turned up with the toolbox and she let me in. Even in her own apartment she wore the hat with the black veil. The shutters were closed; the room was cool and shadowy. She showed me to the bathroom to repair the basin drain. I got down to undo the siphon and she stayed close, her bare knees level with my eyes.

While I struggled with the spanner, she started gently nudging me with them. My mouth was watering and I needed to spit. She put her hand in my hair and tousled it. I stopped working and stayed still. She tightened her grasp on my hair and started pulling me up with it. I obeyed, dropping the spanner.

She turned off the light and pushed her stomach against mine. Her arms came up around my neck and she cradled it, bending it gently towards her face. She opened my mouth with two fingers, then with her lips. I raised my hands in response. She took them and put them behind her back. Then she fumbled for my cock. I was standing against the sink. She pushed against me and my cock entered her. She moved me around. It was more wonderful than being inside the cloud. She put my hands on her breasts and began breathing heavily, faster and faster until the thrust that drained every drop of my blood. There'd been a transfusion from me to her. This had to be the 'making love' that men and women talk about.

I was sweating, my pants right down at my feet and my back stiff from withstanding her movements without the support of the sink. She edged away from me, turned on the light and washed between her legs. She told me to do the same. I picked up my tools.

'If I need you, I'll call you.'

'Yes, madam.'

And that was my first repair job.

The second time was that much easier. Not in the bathroom, but straight to her room. She undressed me, laid me down on her bed and climbed on top of me. She was the one who moved. We stayed together for longer.

Don Gaetano asked me if I was OK about it. I nodded: *yes*.

'She's traded me for you.'

I said it wasn't fair.

'It's fair, and it's also right. She's young and I couldn't respond to all her calls.'

I could. She had various fantasies. One was total darkness. I had to hide, and she'd come in to find me. I'd stay for an hour and then go back down. I'd go up in the afternoon, and this went on till autumn began, when she stopped wearing mourning. She took off her veil and went out wearing colours. The calls stopped coming. It was Don Gaetano who'd recommended me, telling her I was trustworthy, someone who wouldn't talk.

'You needed a taste of nature. Now that you've experienced it, you might even run into the girl from the third floor.'

'And how would I recognize her? Ten years have passed, a bundle of time!'

'*Guaglio*', time isn't a bundle. It's more like a forest. If you know the leaf, you recognize the tree. If you've looked into her eyes, you'll find her again. Even if a forest of time has passed.'

I got the hang of the repairs. I learned quickly. Once I saw something done, I could do it again by myself. I started earning a bit. I understood pipes and wires, knew how to keep the flow inside the conduits, how to keep things moving between bends and switches. I liked being stationmaster of these currents. Being in charge of the water and electricity was like playing, but it wasn't such fun when the outflow got blocked and I had to remove the excrement. The first time, I vomited into it. After that, Don Gaetano got me to tie a handkerchief over my mouth and nose.

Autumn had begun. It was my last year of school. I studied at night and stayed in the lodge during the afternoon, partly for the game but also to stand in for Don Gaetano.

There was one afternoon when nobody needed us for anything. The drizzle was coming down soft and sticky from low clouds. We were playing a hand of *scopa*. I had my back to the windows when Don Gaetano got up to deal with someone who'd come into the lodge. I took advantage of the interruption to go to the loo. I came back to find two girls in raincoats sitting at the table with Don Gaetano. One of them was looking around, the other not. One was blonde and confident, talking with Don Gaetano, the other not. I stood off to the side.

The blonde was asking if there were any vacant apartments in the building. Don Gaetano took his time. He wanted to know whom he was dealing with. He offered them a coffee. They accepted and took off their macs. He put the coffee pot on the burner. Out of habit I never look girls in the face. If I do, I get embarrassed.

'We don't put out For Rent signs here, we just pass the word around. At the moment there aren't any, but there should be one with three rooms coming up on the third floor.'

Don Gaetano paused. I stood at the cooker, looking out of the corner of my eye at the girl who hadn't said anything yet. I was looking at her hair, smooth and chestnut-coloured, like *marron glacé*, gathered in a slide at the nape of her neck.

'It's the house you lived in as a child,' said Don Gaetano, and he smiled a little at the silent girl. I took a step backwards and bumped into the coffee pot, which wouldn't fall.

'Anna.' The word escaped me, but the blonde drowned out my voice, asking if they could see the apartment. Anna turned round very slowly and looked at me, her eyes large and calm, like those of someone behind a window.

'Watch the coffee, *guaglio*' – it's boiling.'

I turned round and tipped over the coffee pot as I took it from the flame.

'Go up and see if the *signorine* can look at the apartment.'

I left like a sleepwalker, my mouth hanging open. As I climbed the stairs, I relived the past, all those times when I'd dared to listen at that door hoping to hear something, hoping to see her come out. It had never happened. And now I was about to knock on her door in order to take her back up there. The past was a staircase, and I was climbing it once more.

I came back to find four cups, one for me too.

'If you go with them, Don Gaetano, the *signorine* can go up.' I drank my coffee, unable to raise my eyes. The window separating the little girl from the world had fallen, and its fragments must have been on the ground.

While they went up to the apartment, I washed the cups and then went out of the lodge and into the courtyard to stand in the rain. I'd dived on to the wet pavement so many times, dodging kicks and feet to grab the ball. I looked at the pipe I used to climb straight up, passing by the first-floor balcony. Now there were pots living on it, containing the last basil of the year.

I leaned back until I could see the third floor. There she was, behind the window, looking down. My eyes dropped down and the coffee came back up my throat, forced by a hiccup. I went back into the lodge, into the loo, and vomited.

They came down, and the blonde asked Don Gaetano to let her know when the contract expired as they were ready to take it over. Anna followed, looking all around her. I helped them put on their macs. The blonde threw her hair over her collar, and I stepped back so as not to get it in my face. Anna kept hers inside her collar, a line in the middle dividing the two sides. The scent of rain rose to my nose, stolen from her shoulders. The weather had put on that scent so I'd recognize it.

She thanked me for my bit of help, turned and shook my hand. She noticed my wound from the oars, and smiled. In our contact there was a childish promise to see each other again next day. Then she shook Don Gaetano's hand. The blonde had already left. It wasn't raining outside anymore.

'Are they coming to live here?'

'I don't think so. They only wanted to visit. The other one was dragged along by the blonde, who talks like a lawyer.'

'I've waited so long to see her I'd forgotten what she might be like. Waiting made me forget what I was waiting for. Is that possible, Don Gaetano, something so absurd?'

'At the orphanage, I waited to be old enough to leave. Then the day came, and I forgot that I'd been waiting for it.'

'I didn't think she'd be so beautiful. Yet she wasn't forward. Pensive, a bit knocked about, like someone who's come home after a journey. Do you think she'll come back?'

'I don't think it. I know it.'

We didn't play *scopa*. I couldn't concentrate. We were distracted by a bit of a brouhaha: a visit from the tax inspector. He'd come to deliver an assessment, a citation to the cobbler La Capa, the guy who'd picked four winning numbers in the Naples lottery two years before. He was officious and self-important, a state functionary who spoke with a northern accent. But getting La Capa to understand something in standard Italian was beyond him.

I go to call the cobbler and I tell him he has a visitor in the lodge. He comes and this encounter follows, which I immediately wrote down in my notebook.

'You are Signor La Capa?

'At your service, Excellency.'

'I have here a citation for you.'

The cobbler puts on a caring look, and tells the official to sit down so he can bring him a glass of water.

'I'm sorry that you're feeling this agitation about me,' and meanwhile he touches him, encouraging him to sit.

'What agitation? What are you talking about? Signor La Capa, I have here a *citation*.'

The cobbler had decided that the man was agitated. He handed him a glass of water.

'But I'm not thirsty, Signor La Capa. Let's not waste time. I'm here from the Minister of Finance.'

'Well done! And who is your fiancée?'

'No one! I'm here about the *imposte*, your taxes.'

'Ah, so you're an imposter?'

'How dare you say that!' The poor man was irritated, and also intimidated because La Capa was holding on to his hands – small trowels stuck on the end of two overgrown arms.

'You see? You're agitated.'

He makes to get up and La Capa gently pushes him back in his seat. Don Gaetano stood there watching everything imperturbably. The cobbler tried to explain himself.

'Listen, Signor Imposter of the *Imposte*: the guy who checks tickets on the tram is called the ticket inspector, no? You are in the *imposte* and so you're an imposter.'

'Look, Signor La Capa, this is verging on the outrageous.'

'*Ma quanno mai*, how can that be? No one's outraged here. But you're much too pale. You look like someone from Bellomunno, the guy who does the funerals. Don't you think so, Don Gaetano? He's wearing the black shoes one wears for funerals.'

'Now you've gone too far.' The poor inspector makes as if to get up, but La Capa hammers him down on the chair with the stroke of someone nailing the sole on a shoe. The inspector realizes he's in trouble and starts looking around for help. Don Gaetano is a Sphinx.

'So will you get it into your head that I am an income tax inspector?'

'Ah no, if you're going to be disrespectful, then don't come in!'

'But Signor La Capa, perhaps you're deaf!'

'Me? Deaf?! When I can hear what's being said by the flies in Piazza Municipio all the way up here? You're the one who speaks like a foreigner.'

'I speak normal Italian.'

'Well, no, with my *nonna*, we could speak only Neapolitan.'

The inspector feels defeated. He draws a hand through his thinning hair and clams up, hardly daring to move to get up.

'Have a glass of water,' orders La Capa.

He obeys, eyes closed. Don Gaetano finally intervenes before he starts crying. 'I'll see to the collector, La Capa. Go back to your apartment.'

'Yes, yes! You look after him. I haven't understood a thing he was saying, that foreigner.'

Don Gaetano takes delivery of the citation and lets the inspector go.

'We won't see that one again.'

'Don Gaetano, if you'd waited one more minute, we'd have had to take him to the hospital!'

'He deserved his run-in with La Capa. The moment some poor soul has a bit of good luck, the state turns up to take it off him. La Capa was right. The guy was wearing black shoes like you do for a funeral.'

For the rest of the afternoon, Don Gaetano taught me how to put hemp around threaded pipes and to grease the joints between pipes to seal them. I hadn't used a threader before, the tool for cutting and threading pipes. He made me try it a couple of times and I got it.

'I have to redo an installation – I'm going on Sunday. If you want to come along and give me a hand, we'll have it done before noon and we'll split the pay.'

'Split it? No way. You're the one with experience – I'm only an assistant. If you give me 10 per cent I'll be fine.'

'I'll give you a quarter and that's the end of the discussion.'

And that's how it went. On the following Sunday, from seven in the morning till twelve noon on the dot, we redid the installation. I went back home at two and bumped into Anna in front of the door, which was closed. Don Gaetano had insisted that I wash my face and hands, and I could shake hers without getting it dirty.

'Will you let me in?' She was a bit rushed and kept looking around.

I opened the door without trembling, but my throat was tight. I couldn't possibly take her to the little room I slept in – it was too small for two. I went into the lodge. In those few rooms was a door I'd never opened, but I knew that behind it were the stairs going down. I opened it – it had to lead to the hiding place. I stopped holding my breath long enough to ask her to follow me.

I lit a candle and started the descent. Anna put her hand on my shoulder, so heavy that its pressure made me teeter. The silence of the tufa opened and closed round our footsteps.

We came to the large room I'd entered ten years before. I set the candle on a ledge overhead. We stayed still as sparks from the candle confettied her forehead, her hair. Her eyes sparkled in answer to the light. My breathing was still and didn't stir the air. I told her I hadn't been down there since then.

'Everything in the *palazzo* is smaller than I remember it when I was a child. Except for you.'

Her voice moved through time. It began as a child's and finished as an adult's. When she got to the 'tu', she touched my arm, and I followed her hand as she lifted it to her shoulder. My other arm found its own way around her waist. It was the starting pose of a dance.

'Here we are, just the way I've always imagined it. You climbed up the balcony to see me and I came downstairs to meet you. You had a tower with a dungeon where we'd dance. Children's desires are the future's commands. The future is a slow but loyal servant.'

Anna spoke without a trace of an accent. It was the language of books, their cherished lines on her breath. She stopped as if to start a new paragraph. It was my turn.

'I waited until I forgot what I was waiting for. A sense of expectation has stayed with me and it greets me when I wake and jump out of bed to meet the day. I open the door, not to go out but to let the day in.'

I rested my head against hers. 'Anna, an eternity has passed.'

'It's over. Time begins now, and will last only moments.'

'Every day I hoped the ball would land on the abandoned balcony. I'd climb up sustained by the thought that you were watching me. And then, still on the terrace, after I threw the ball down so they'd stop looking at me, I'd try to find your face in the window. We should have got married then, as kids. How did you manage to recognize me?'

She took her head from mine and looked at my profile by candlelight.

'I need a kiss before I can answer you.'

With dry lips I moved towards hers, smooth and barely parted. First, I drew a litre of heady oxygen through my nose. Then Anna's breath mingled with mine. Starved of breath, my body rushed towards her lips to regain its balance.

'Do you hear the same thing? Wax sealing a letter?'

I heard Anna's words through my nose. They hadn't passed through her voice or my ears. Can you hear thoughts through your nose? And you, Anna, can you hear mine?

Her lips gave the answer, parting from mine to say 'Yes'.

Nothing else happened with our bodies. We were already overflowing from our lips and the breath we drew in through our

noses mixed with our thoughts. We'd paid our debt to childhood. We'd fulfilled our childish desires: for a dance in the dungeon and a kiss. The exhaustion before the finish line came over
us. We sat down side by side on the camp bed, illuminated by
the blaze of the candle. I got up to lower it and set it on the
floor. I sat down again.

'I'm not beside you, Anna, I *am* your side.'

'You're the missing part that comes back to fit with the other
after being faraway.'

The light rose from our feet and spread its heat across our
faces.

'This isn't a candle, it's a forest fire,' she said.

Anna took my hand and put it in her lap. 'We don't have any
more time – we've run out – and we're snatching extra.'

'Then can I trade the end for the beginning? The first kiss for
the last?'

'You can't count kisses, my side. It wasn't Kiss Number One,
but maybe the thousandth of all the kisses I was waiting for. No
kiss is the first one; they're all seconds. I gave you the first one
from behind the window the day you climbed up to the balcony.
You scaled the precipice for me. I let you have my first time then.'

She squeezed my fingers, still stinging with blisters.

'And this is another second kiss, because even our hands
embrace and kiss.'

'Your eyes are like the curves on the keel of a boat, Anna.'

'My eyes don't sleep and don't cry.'

What is it that separates us? And what time is about to end?

The thought met its answer.

'The gangster I'm promised to gets out of prison soon. He
wants to marry me and leave for South America.'

'I have no right to know. If I could, I'd ask why I never saw
you outside the window.'

Anna's response was to disentangle herself from me and put her hands on her knees. 'I was disturbed as a child, closed up inside. I couldn't cry, even when they slapped me. These days they'd call me autistic. I'm crazy, my side, someone who orders her dreams and desires around. I'm Queen of the Witches' Blood, the blood of those who were burned in the squares. See how that candle yearns for me?

'They took me away and put me in a clinic in the mountains. I never saw my family again. But I inherited from them. When I was eighteen, I left the clinic and came back here. I didn't remember where the *palazzo* was. I'm living in a hotel. I've been looking for this place and for that window for a year now. I wanted to remember what I saw. And instead, I remembered what I'd never heard: you, saying my name. My name, in the mouth of a boy who was making coffee in a porter's lodge. I remembered it despite never having heard it before. I'm made of leaves, like a tree, and I recognize a wind even if it has never blown. So it was easy to look from behind the window and find you there again. It was you, a sapling grown up where I'd left it. You, too, are made of wood, for burning and to sail in.'

I trembled beside the candle.

'Are you afraid? Yes . . . tremble, my side. Your trembling is only a down-payment. Go on, tremble. Here in this dungeon, you can tremble in safety.'

She caressed my burning forehead with icy fingers. Her gesture calmed my fears like a cloth wiping away dust.

The wick was throwing out sparks. Anna grabbed one of them and put it to her tongue.

'Do you think the stars taste like icing or are they salty?'

'I don't know. I've never tasted them.'

'Well, I do. I stayed out on the balcony many nights in the

home for disturbed children. In summer, the stars drop crumbs
that land in your mouth.'

'And what are they like?'

'Salty. They taste of bitter almonds.'

'I'd prefer them sweet.'

'Oh no! There are so many of them they'd damage the earth.
On some nights there are storms of crumbling stars. The earth
is sown with them, and it receives them without being able to
give anything back. Then the animals and trees from below
offer up prayers in exchange, saying "thank you".'

'Do you pray, Anna?'

'No.'

'Why not?'

'Because that's where I come from. From a seed carried on
the icy tail of a comet.'

'And you came *here* to be born, in the narrowest and loudest
streets in the world?'

'Yes. The comets' lost tail ends up in the mouth of the volca-
noes. My seed dropped into the crater, and the eruption of 1944
spat me out. From the tufa in this dungeon I'm breathing in the
stuff of my origins.'

'Me too, Anna, I'm the son of the tufa in this place. I don't
come from outer space, like you, but from inside a courtyard. I
lifted up my eyes not to the heavens, but to your window, which
was a step from heaven fallen to earth. My breath rose to your
window and fogged it up. You dried it with your sleeve. I love the
glass of the windows, for in it I saw you, your head in your hands.
And the windows in the courtyard threw a reflection of your
image down to my *stanzino*. It was a relay; if one of them was
missing, your image got lost in the air. I'm thankful for the courtyard windows. And what do I do now that you've come down
from the windows – with this happiness? What can I do, Anna?'

She started. 'Do? What a strange thought! You think there's something to *do* between us? There aren't any verbs here, only our names, and nothing to add to them. There's a bed, and we've neither lain nor embraced on it. It's as dry as an altar before a sacrifice.'

'Do you want to lie down?'

'Not now, my side. This bed is a wound that needs dressing. I'll bring sheets.' She got up, and so did I. She took my hand and moved towards the stairs. I gathered up the candle and followed her. Instead of feet I had a swallow's tail, fluttering with the joy of soaring in the air once more.

I walked her to the door. It was massive, and you had to give it a shove with your shoulders. I didn't have the strength to open it and separate us.

She opened it with one arm, effortlessly. From her slight body came a violent, compressed energy. The door moved as easily as a curtain. Anna's breathy 'See you Sunday' hit me along with the squeak of the hinges. She'd already turned away.

I stayed behind the closed door. My boyhood wish had been fulfilled. Of all the things I'd longed for, I'd clung to the most fantastic: Anna's kiss. I hadn't missed what one has as a child: a family. I'd gone without, like so many after the war. I didn't feel melancholy about it. On the contrary, I'd had the freedom to do my own thing during the day, without a clock. I had my little room, school, the courtyard. I had soup brought to me by my adoptive mother's maid. She'd kept me from the orphanage, where I was destined to go. Out of my whole childhood, I chose the little girl at the window as the thing I most needed. When she disappeared from it, my world shrank to a cage. I had to live without the freedom to raise my eyes. Now, ten years later, Anna had come all the way down from the third floor to the dungeon for our wedding as children. Time was a letter, sealed with a kiss.

Anna was crazy. What did it mean? Don Gaetano came in while I was still standing dazed behind the door. I told him immediately that I'd misused the lodge and that I'd also opened the door to the stairs going down. I hadn't had anywhere to take Anna.

'You did the right thing, *guaglio'*. Don't worry about it.'

'Don Gaetano, did you know that Anna was crazy?'

'They treated her as if she were. She didn't want to speak, didn't want contact with anyone. They sent her to a clinic – they were ashamed of her. The whole time she was here, she never went outside.'

'She says she's crazy.'

'The ones who are don't know it and they don't tell you.'

'Why does she say that?'

We'd gone into the lodge and Don Gaetano had started cutting up vegetables.

'At an age when you're very emotional, the heart isn't big enough to withstand the blood pumping through it. The world around you is tiny compared to the grandeur filling your breast. At that age, a woman has to shrink to fit the world. The conflict inside her leads her to believe she can't do it – that it would take too much violence to shrink.

'It's a risky age. Women undergo a kind of physical apotheosis we can't possibly understand. We can exalt ourselves for a woman; they exalt themselves through the force contained within them. It's the ancient energy of the priestesses, guardians of the flame.'

I helped him clean potatoes. His words about Anna made sense, but didn't fit all of her.

'What should I do?'

'Take only a thin layer. You shouldn't throw any of the potato away. It should be like the wood that curls up when you use a plane.'

'What should I do about Anna?'

'You should meet up with her; you should get to know her in order to stop thinking about her. She's not for you. But you won't be free if you don't get to know her.'

'I don't want to be free. I want to be shut up in a room with her.'

We put the vegetables on to boil and played *scopa*. Each time the cards were dealt, the odd cards came out even. *Scopa* was a game that induced peace.

My trousers hadn't bulged with Anna. Over the summer it had happened quickly; the widow got to me there. But with Anna it hadn't happened. The kiss brought blood to my lips. My mouth smelled of it. Anna made my ears ring, my nose dry, my lips burn. She made me thirsty. A fever rose and fell in me throughout the day. I drank water so I wouldn't shrivel up.

I studied at night, as usual. I enjoyed Latin, a language devised by some puzzle-setter. Translating it was like looking for the solution. I didn't like the accusative case – it had an ugly name. The dative was lovely, the vocative theatrical, and the ablative essential. It was lazy of Italian to have given up its cases. In history I grew bored with the three little wars of independence, but I was intrigued by the story of the south's resistance, which was classified as banditry. The winners always have to denigrate the losers. The south remained fond of its defeats. It was a much bloodier military epic than the skirmishes of the Risorgimento, with the odd double battles of Custoza, lost twice over the years. I didn't like Cavour, and Mazzini was the founder of an armed gang. Garibaldi arrived at a lucky moment, Pisacane at just the wrong one. History was like the ingredients in cooking: change the quantities and you had another dish.

I couldn't play the same game with chemistry or physics. Atoms had divvied up the world peacefully, but there'd been a period of war between oxygen and hydrogen before they came to an agreement over the formula for water. Water is a peace treaty. Chemistry was the study of the equilibrium achieved by the world's matter.

I hardly had anything to do with my classmates. I helped out with assignments in class, but I didn't bother talking to anyone, including the teachers. I answered, and that was that. On Saturday afternoons I was summoned to play football.

A goalie is a viewpoint. He has to predict and pre-empt the shot from his spot. When there's danger in front of goal, he has to throw himself into the tangle of feet. He pays dearly for the advantage of using his hands. I was more daring because I didn't give a damn about myself. They entrusted me with the defence, the noblest duty, and I honoured it. Allowing a goal was failure. Unstoppable goals don't exist: they are errors of positioning in anticipating the shot. I blocked penalties, though not those kicked with the left foot. Lefties are less predictable. Their feet have whims governed not by their brains, but by the feet themselves. I'm a leftie too.

Both at school and in football my interaction was limited to throw-ins. I put the ball back in play, and I did the same with questions. I was a bit autistic myself, but without Anna's extremism. She was made to be inside a fortress, warding off the siege.

I continued to lose at *scopa*, three games out of three. Even if I had a lucky hand, drew the *settebello*, the seven of coins, and got the highest prime, Don Gaetano managed to make up for it, playing the cards he'd seen. He didn't read my thoughts, didn't use that advantage. He calculated probabilities.

'Don Gaetano, when can I have the honour of playing a game with you?'

The count showed up at the lodge and invited himself to our table.

'You're hopeless at *scopa*. No offence! Play with the kid here and if you win, we'll have a game.'

The count settled for playing the qualifying round with me. One of us had to reach eleven points, and he lost.

'The cards want me to lose!' . . . 'What a spiteful game.' . . . 'I can't even leave cards on the table because he has the card needed to sweep them up.' He grew irritated and left, saying goodbye only to Don Gaetano.

His aftershave made you sneeze.

'That cloud of cologne fogs up his brain. Of course he's going to lose at *scopa*!' When the count left, Don Gaetano opened the window and waved a rag around in the air to clear it.

Don Gaetano hummed a song he'd learned on the ship that took him to Argentina.

> *Me ne vogl'i' lontano tanto tanto*
> *che nun m'ha da truva' manco lo viento*
> *che nun m'ha da truva' manco lo viento*
> *manco lo sole che cammina tanto.*

> *I want to go far, far away*
> *So no one can find me, not even the wind*
> *So no one can find me, not even the wind*
> *Not even the sun, which travels far.*

It was the nursery rhyme of a young peasant from the Marches who'd been in the next bunk over in the hold. After all his twenty years in Argentina, Don Gaetano remembered the voyage and the ocean. The wish of the boy who'd scaled the orphanage gate to go and see the lighted ships at anchor in the bay had been fulfilled.

'A voyage is something you make by sea, in a ship – not in a train. The horizon must be empty and should separate sea and sky. There can't be anything around, and the immensity must bear down on you. That's a voyage.

'Some of them cried. Although misery had compelled them to go, still their loss gnawed at them. Apart from a few – the worst ones – no one had any spirit of adventure. The money for their tickets had been collected from several families' savings. It was an investment in the future, and the return would be the success of their relative, whose alarm at this overwhelming duty, the obligation to make a fortune, was as unnerving as the sea was vast. I told the ones who were crying that the sea was growing ever wider with the addition of their salty water. This voyage was meant to make them forget their point of departure. It lasted about a month, and at the end the men disembarked ready, their heads held high, noses in the air.'

And that Saturday I broke my nose. I'd thrown myself between all those feet to grab the ball. I was just in time but in the heat of the race, the other guy kicked anyway and got me in the face. I didn't let go. The referee whistled a foul. When I put my hand to my nose I discovered it had shifted. It must have looked awful. The others were staring at me in alarm. A medical student took it between his fingers and straightened it with one brisk movement. The cartilage had been derailed and he put it back in place. He told me there was an indentation in the bone, a partial fracture. They put in a substitute and I held some ice to my nose to slow down the bleeding.

At the end of the game, my opponent came to apologize. I remembered a phrase from Don Gaetano's stories and I said: 'These sorts of things happen the day before.'

'The day before what?'

'The day before happiness.'

He went off, shaking his head.

I returned home with swollen, purple eyes. Don Gaetano made me a compress of salty water.

I slept, aching, in a flurry of dreams, and woke up while it was still dark. I felt nothing in my nose. It was plugged up with dried blood. I didn't want to lose my nose around Anna. I wrapped a bit of loo paper around the shell of a biro and tried to open a passage through my nostrils with it. The pain forced tears out of me. I tried dissolving the clot with hot water, and it came out rose-coloured. Is that what they call rosewater?

I tricked myself out of the pain by thinking about Anna. I blew through my nostrils, but my breath came back in my throat. With all the prodding and rinsing, the plug gave way and I started bleeding all over again. Smells could get up there, and the scent of her *marron glacé* hair was the one I wanted. I spent the rest of the day rinsing my nostrils in hot water to stop them clotting.

'Don Gaetano, I'm a chimney sweep.'

'Leave your poor nose alone.'

I insisted on working that day. 'It's my snout that's beaten up, not my arms.' It was light work, putting in a new electrical system. Just wires to thread through ducts so they could be connected. We'd finished by noon.

The steam from the *minestra* surprised me. It smelled of blood. I chewed on some bread with olives. Don Gaetano insisted that I drink a glass of wine. 'The wine makes up for the blood you've lost.'

Yes, it balanced things out. At an *osteria*, though, it went beyond balancing things out and made you lose your balance instead. Don Gaetano went there in the evenings for a bit of company, and he'd always return holding up someone who'd overdone it.

'Last night the guy leaning on me vomited up a litre in the street. They drink without eating anything, and what little money they have goes on wine without a morsel of bread to eat with it. He apologized to me. "It's nothing," I told him, "but I'm sorry for you, since you're emptier now than you were before." The *osteria* is better than the theatre – every table's a comedy. No tragedies – they only put on light fare. The ones with serious problems don't go.'

After we'd eaten he put his coat on and went out, saying he'd be back late.

'When you've finished what you have to do, close up the lodge and I'll see you tomorrow.'

The silence he left behind him when the door closed, the silence of a Sunday afternoon, scalded my ears. I put my cold palms over them and tried breathing through my nose. There was an airway but I rinsed it all the same in lukewarm water. Out came the rosewater again.

I wasn't unhappy about having broken my nose the day before. Someone called to defend the goal is responsible for the whole team. The day before the liberation, Don Gaetano went to fight with the Neapolitans. He didn't stay in his house, waiting. He'd done what was necessary, and so had I. What if the liberation had found him dead the next day? It would have been worse if it had found him hiding. Freedom must be earned and defended. Not happiness: that's a gift, which has nothing to do with whether or not someone is a good goalie and blocks penalties. Happiness – was it right to name it without knowing it? It sounded shameless in my mouth, like when someone shows off about knowing a celebrity and just uses their first name, saying Marcello when they really mean Mastroianni.

Of Anna and of happiness I knew only the name. If she didn't come, where would I look for it? I shouldn't have allowed myself such familiarity. When she comes, I'll be able to say what it is, this famous 'happiness'.

I took my hands off my ears. My thoughts had been warming them. The silence was gone. From one balcony came the voice of the radio, from another the rattling of crockery. I had to wash ours, and I did, before going out into the courtyard. Overhead, the clouds were climbing. The pavement was wet with dripping clothes. The wind had come up and I was stung with melancholy, the melancholy of a day that was slipping away. I imagined the sunset, the sun going down beneath the hills, dragging lengthening clouds behind it. I went out into the street. I didn't expect Anna at any particular time. There was only a scrap left of the whole day of happiness.

If she didn't come, what would I call that day? I wouldn't call it anything. It would just be a normal one, with all the things I had to do, including studying a bit of Greek. But I didn't like Plato. He'd started writing the Socratic dialogues – and what gave him the right? Had he taken notes every evening like I do with Don Gaetano's stories, or did he call them up from memory? Plato cheated, putting his own views in his master's mouth and in those of others. He hid behind them. Is that what a writer does? He shouldn't do that. A writer should be smaller than his subject. He must realize that the story escapes him from every side, and he collects only part of it. People who read have a taste for the abundance that overtakes a writer.

With Plato, though, the story stays completely enclosed within his fence. He doesn't let a flicker of independent life escape it. His dialogues are marshalled in lines: two by two, question and answer, 'Forward march!'

This thought came to me as I watched the boys in military academy uniform coming out of the Nunziatella two by two. At my age – when they might have been at high school – they were studying at the military academy. As they descended towards Santa Lucia, Anna's bouncy gait countered the stream. She broke the rows of two, crossing in the middle. The boys moved apart and she went between the lines. She walked up, head held high, her flowered dress clinging to her, tinfoil round a bouquet. She was carrying a package in her arms, and her hair, just washed, swung to the rhythm of her steps.

I blew through my nose, trying to catch her scent from afar. It was early evening and the streetlamps were just lighting up. They couldn't illuminate anything yet, but they made her smile in response. She was dressed lightly for an autumn evening, and the high heels she was wearing pushed her whole body forward. She'd put on make-up.

'Let me in.' She looked behind her.

We went through the door quickly, into the lodge. My head started throbbing violently and the pain in my nose tolled like a bell. In the kitchen she turned to give me the packet: it was bedsheets. She took my face between her hands and pushed her mouth, coloured pink, against mine, breathing deeply. It was a delectable pain, a stab in the eyes, chocolate melting in the mouth. At that moment she noticed the swelling around my nose.

'What have you done?'

'Got kicked, yesterday.'

She didn't ask anything else. 'I brought sheets.' And she

started for the door that opened on to the stairway going down. I lit the candle and closed the door on the city behind us.

We went down to a place where no one would find us. Anna followed me, her hand on my neck. From her body came a strength that made the air tremble.

The kiss had been violent, the hold on my neck was tight. At the bottom of the stairs, I set the candle on the ground. She made the bed. I watched her moving around. Rather than doing things herself, she gave orders to things and they followed them. She shook the first sheet in the air and it flew over the mattress, so that she only had to tuck it in. The same with the second sheet and the bedspread. She came closer and started to undress me. My jacket was already off, and the buttons on my shirt opened by themselves at her prompting. She took my shirt off me in one swift movement that made the flame wobble, and me too. She put her ear against my tight chest, hollowed out at the ribs, and squeezed my sides. I couldn't breathe.

'Easy, Anna, you'll snap me in two.'

'Quiet. I'm listening to your blood. It's full of air.'

She took off my belt, and I was so skinny that my trousers fell down by themselves. She pushed me down on the bed and took off my socks and shoes. I was naked and I slipped under the sheets. She took off nothing, not even her shoes, and got under the covers.

I was between her and the wall. She lay on top of me, her small breasts spread over my chest and her arms closed around my shoulders, trapping me. She wasn't using any force, but I couldn't move. Even my legs were caught between hers. I could breathe, but only if she wasn't squeezing me. I couldn't imagine such effortless strength. Are all women like this during happiness? Can their embrace crush you? The widow wasn't like that. I was the one who held her.

Anna buried her head between my neck and shoulder, nuzzling me with her lips and teeth. Heat passed from her to me: moist, burning. In my nose I smelled blood mixed with the cinnamon of her *marron glacé* hair. The deeper she buried her head against my neck, the more I gave in. I'd stopped noticing that I was hardly breathing. My prick swelled. I stretched my neck to make more space for her inside me. For a space of time I couldn't measure, she was a climber winding around the balcony. Our sexes were separated by her dress and they fitted together. Hers went wild. She held me in her arms; they cracked. A few short snarls escaped her before a bite that called the pain from my nose to make it course through my neck. Then she licked me there.

'Did I hurt you?'

'No.'

'Are you scared?'

'Yes.'

'Of me?'

'Yes. And courage will never be as lovely as this fear.'

Anna lifted her head from my neck. Her mouth was smeared with red. The candlelight coloured her forehead with a sunset, the strands of her hair long clouds drawn after it. She looked at me, her eyes wide open, and brought her bloody lips to mine, pushed her mouth inside mine until I could feel it in my throat. My prick was a plank stuck to her stomach. She eased the pressure of the kiss, broke off. With a swerve of her hips, she turned me over and I was on top of her. She unwound her arms from my shoulders and guided my hands to her breasts. Opened her legs, pulled up her dress and, holding my hips over her, pushed my prick against her opening. I was her plaything, which she moved around. Our sexes were ready, poised in expectation, barely touching each other: ballet dancers hovering *en pointe*.

We stayed like that. Anna looked down at them. She pushed

65

on my hips, an order that thrust me in. I entered her. Not only my prick, but the whole of me entered her, into her guts, into her darkness, eyes wide open, seeing nothing. My whole body had gone inside her. I went in with her thrusts and stayed still. While I got used to the quiet and the pulsing of my blood in my ears and nose, she pushed me out a little, then in again. She did it again and again, holding me with force and moving me to the rhythm of the surf. She wiggled her breasts beneath my hands and intensified the pushing. I went in up to my groin and came out almost entirely. My body was her gearstick. She wasn't breathing. Her eyes seemed faraway.

'Anna,' I called, chained to her movements.

'*Sì, sì.*' From her lips came perfect syllables. I called her to make her breathe. I called her to hear: '*Sì.*' Her 'yes' called me and I was about to say it too when with one thrust I sank into her without coming back out. She took her hands from my hips and from my prick came the entire 'yes' that had coursed through her. The 'yes' of my emptying and my goodbye, my welcome, the 'yes' of a marionette that flops without a hand to hold its strings. I moved to the side and saw the blood-stained bed.

'It's ours. The ink of our pact. You put your initial inside me and I waited for it, intact. I'll give it a body and a name.'

'Anna, in your hands, I know what I'm for. I'm made for this.'

She kissed the tips of my lips, put her tongue between them. 'You have a nice taste. I had to hold back from eating you.' She wasn't smiling.

'Can I kiss you?'

'No. You're pollen. Obey me, for I am the wind.'

Is this happiness, letting yourself be caught? Anna rose and got on top of me.

She held my arms firmly between her legs. She put the

fingers of her right hand around my throat and with her left hand she caressed my face. She started tightening her grip.

'Would you die for me? Would you die for Crazy Anna?'

Pinned beneath her, I managed to nod '*Sì.*'

She continued caressing me with one hand and clutching my throat with the other.

'Would you die for me, under me?'

Only my eyes could say '*Sì*'. I wasn't breathing and I wasn't defending myself. She kept squeezing me. I shut my eyes and everything went white.

I came to in the dark, with the candle spent and Anna gone. Blindly, I searched for my clothes, got dressed and crawled up the stairs. The light upstairs was like a slap in the eyes. I saw what time it was: nine at night. Don Gaetano hadn't come back. I went into my little room and washed myself. I was smeared with red all over. The pain in my nose was beside the point. My throat burned where she'd strangled me. I took a sip of water that wouldn't go down. I swallowed it in spoonfuls.

I lay down on the bed. It had come, the day of happiness. The most terrible day of my short life.

I missed school the next morning. I couldn't get out of bed. I stopped counting how many bits of me hurt – it took less time to count the ones that weren't damaged. My nose had closed up again and I left it like that. I didn't want to smell anything. I didn't want to feel.

Don Gaetano came by since he hadn't seen me leave. He covered my neck with a handkerchief. He came in and told me he'd bring me something to eat at lunchtime.

'Don't go to the trouble. I'll come. It's only weakness.' It was the weakness that makes you hunker down and gather your forces. I'd read a book on mountaineering, one of Don Raimondo's used books. It talked about the exhaustion you feel when you reach the summit, the impulse to go to sleep there when in fact you've got to descend in order not to be overtaken by the dark a long way from camp. I, too, had to descend from the peak of happiness. I hadn't imagined such an adventure. Anna had been a storm I'd wished would never end. I didn't want the calm to return. How would it help if I took shelter from her? She'd gone away, she'd gone elsewhere to discharge her violent energy. The day after happiness, I was a mountaineer, careering down the slope.

Was I crazy too, or was that the unutterable name of love? When someone said it in films, it was wasted. Yet actors specialized in saying it. They'd studied at the academy, practised before the mirror, appeared before a jury and other audiences in order to say at last: 'I love you.'

It was better written on walls or on the bark of trees. There was more chance that it would make its point. Saying it was just watching your spittle fall on the ground. Saying it was wasting it. Until the preceding scene, love showed up in disguise, hidden behind some gesture of embarrassment, say, a facial tic. But the moment it was declared, it came out, betrayed by the very formula that should have proclaimed it. Every 'I love you' in films was a failure. No one knew how to say it. It was all the more impossible for me, an emotional illiterate, to find my way around the word 'love'. I was simply ready to be Anna's, a body at the service of her every urgent move. I didn't want to come down from the peak I'd climbed. I wanted to stay up there, fluttering like a pennant in the wind.

The thought filled me with energy. I got up out of bed, opened a book and studied. At noon I went to see Don Gaetano. He'd put some vegetables on to cook. 'I've put in ten.' Outside, autumn was rattling the windows. 'The southwest wind – it'll last for three days. It won't let the ships leave. It flings you around if you're already at sea, and anyone on an island is screwed.'

Salty air moved up through the alleyways and the city took on the taste of the sea. Waves jumped over the breakwater formed by the cliffs and swept the seafront.

After lunch we headed out into virgin air, innocent of the earth. Oxygen whipped the crest of the waves. My nose was unblocked by the pressure of the southwest wind, which battered the coats of those who had one, and people who'd come out in their hats had to keep hold of them. We walked from the port to Mergellina, barely speaking. The wind snatched our words away.

' '*O vient*' ' . . . In dialect, the wind was faster and impudent. '*O vient*'. I repeated it while I walked, as I'd done with Anna's name the day before. A light-grey American aircraft carrier floated in the bay, an empty road cut off at poop and prow. It didn't fit in with the rest of the bay or the ships at anchor. Didn't fit in with the swell of the volcano or with the coast, which breached the sea like the back of a whale. The deck of the aircraft carrier was a deserted road opposite the overcrowded city.

After Anna, the wind, with all its force, had the effect of a massage. The sky, ruffled with battered clouds, suddenly threw out a stream of light that dazzled the surf. The sea isn't actually blue. It's white. It has to crash against the cliffs to come out. Nature must be white inside. We're red. The sea, the sky and fire share this secret whiteness, the colour I'd seen beneath Anna's fingers as she gripped my throat.

At Mergellina we went into a bar. Don Gaetano wanted to buy me a coffee. We'd been walking for an hour against the wind, and our faces were chafed, our ears deafened. The little cup of boiling liquid warmed our fingers, our senses properly reunited around the handle. Propped up against the bar, we tasted the coffee at the tip of our lips, two hornets hovering over a flower.

'She's not for you.' The hubbub in the bar and the steam spewing out of the espresso machine confused me, and I didn't immediately grasp what he was saying to me.

'That girl is not for you.'

'You've already said so, and I admit you're right.' I put down my cup. 'I'm no match for her. At the moment, I'm useful to her. For what, I don't know. But I want to be useful in some way. Anna has a power that's hard to resist.'

Don Gaetano looked outside towards the sea. 'Broken noses take care of themselves, but blood doesn't flow back inside. What goes out is lost.'

'What does mine matter? What should I save it for? If she asks for it, it's hers.'

Don Gaetano turned once more towards the bar and drank his last sip of coffee. 'You can do what you like with your own blood, but with someone else's, no.'

I didn't understand and I couldn't ask. Outside, the wind lifted the white off the sea and scattered it over the road, throwing rice at newlyweds.

We left the bar. On the way home, the wind got us from behind, grabbing us by the neck, giving us a few kicks. A huge wave sprayed us. Overcome with glee, I ran for a bit. Don Gaetano adjusted his sopping beret. We were alone – 'o vient' had shut the city up at home. I imagined it abandoned, people having fled, their doors left open and their pots on the fire. I could go into all the buildings, sit in the bishop's and the mayor's chairs, live in the Palazzo Reale, board the ships. Even the Americans had disappeared, leaving the aircraft carrier empty in the middle of the bay. The thought tickled my nose. It lasted until I saw them coming right at us, against the wind. They were running in a group, in T-shirts, shorts and gym shoes. The two of us all wrapped up, them practically naked. The city's residents had vanished and Martians had landed.

Don Gaetano and I looked at our feet to see if we were on earth or in the sky. 'To run' was a serious verb as far as we were concerned. We'd only start running to escape an earthquake or an air raid. Running without being chased was like boiling water without making pasta.

They passed us, concentrating on their movements and puffing into the wind.

'They can't be real, Don Gaetano. We're hallucinating, and the coffee's to blame – it was boiling.'

'But they do exist. They're the last people created on the earth, the last to arrive. They know how to make war and cars. They're a people of overgrown children. If you ask them where they are, they say: far from home. They do exist. For them, we're the ones who don't exist. They cross paths with us, they pass us by, but they don't see us. They live here and they don't even see the volcano. I read in the paper that an American sailor fell into the mouth of Vesuvius. Nothing strange about it. He just didn't see it.'

Once the shore was behind us, our dense crowds reappeared, scattered throughout the alleyways. The elderly moved about unsteadily, looking for somewhere to rest, while children spread their arms, hoping to be caught up by the wind. There was no laundry left outside – it had been hauled in so the gusts wouldn't blow it away. Without the sheets hanging down, you could see the sky above, dotted with puffy clouds and smelling like deep-fried *panzarotti*.

'Do you feel like eating?' Don Gaetano asked, looking up. He'd heard my thoughts about the clouds.

'It's their fault – they've been fried by a pro.'

It was the day of recovery from happiness. Don Gaetano and the wind had taken on the duty of helping me get over Sunday. It was working. That's how I got to know the happiness that's forgotten by the next day. I didn't think about Anna. My bashed-up body was evidence enough of my close shave with happiness.

La Capa was waiting in the lodge to ask Don Gaetano something.

'You studied at the cemetery, right?'

'The *seminary*.'

'That's it. You studied there, right, so did you know there are catacombs in Rome?'

We were confused by La Capa's remarks. I hurried towards the loo. Don Gaetano sat there and took it, but he remained calm.

'I visited them with my wife and my little girl. A long time ago the Christians had to hide there. But the way I see it, Don Gaetano, it was OK that you Christians had to hide in there because you're saints and masticated Christians.'

'Masticated?'

'Er, the ones the lions ate.'

'*Martyred*?'

'That's it. I'm telling you, it's all very well that you're saints and Christian marbles.'

'They became fish. But they're not marbles, or even snappers. They're *martyrs*.'

'OK, fine. But why do they have to crap in the tombs? I took my family there!'

'Did it stink?'

'No, actually not. My wife, excuse my saying so, is ignorant and didn't get it. I felt humiliated and ashamed.'

'They must have put in some sanitation.'

'Of course, but I have to say that it's not a very nice place to show off, those Christian catacombs.'

'With all the places there are to see in Rome, did you have to go there?'

'They drove us there in the couch.'

'And that was the whole trip?'

'No, no. We went to St Peter's and saw the colognes.'

'There's cologne in St Peter's?'

'*Gnernò*, no sir, there's a *row* of colognes, one nearby and another one, too.'

'You mean *columns*?'

'That's it. They were so pretty! White as shoe cream. So I came down to find out from you, since you were there in that place, when you were studying in that cemetery, if they told you there were catacombs in Rome.'

'I'm finding out about it here and now from you.'

And so off he went, the cobbler La Capa, marvelling after his outing to Rome.

'Don Gaetano, you have some control to keep from laughing in La Capa's face. You're a hero!'

'On the contrary, he scares me! If he sees someone's taking the mickey out of him, he'll break their bones. Be careful not to let him see you so much as smirk. You'll never be able to defend yourself.'

'That's why I have to go and hide as soon as he shows up. But I always listen to everything. I stuff a rag in my mouth and stay there listening.'

We played *scopa*, finished our soup, and I drank a whole glass of wine from Ischia. Don Gaetano was treating me differently. He hadn't called me '*guaglio*', 'kid', the whole day. After supper he started up again with his stories about the war.

'We were used to hearing lies on the radio or in the papers:

73

about the homeland, the heroic defence of the borders, the empire. We had the empire – we didn't have any bread or coffee, but we had the empire.

'When the Americans arrived, that very radio and the same newspapers took their side. From one day to the next, the enemy became the liberator. The same newspapers and the articles penned by the same journalists now said the opposite. It was like you were reading upside-down. Turks had become Christians, no one was Fascist and they never had been. Their rule was to save their jobs. But there were so many changes that this was just window-dressing. Suddenly there was white bread. The Americans distributed flour to the bakers who hadn't had any for years. And along with the white bread came the black soldiers. No one in the city had ever seen any. The old folks in the street were constantly crossing themselves.'

Don Gaetano's stories opened up my ears. His metallic voice plucked the strings of my imagination. It's how I tasted the first white bread out of the ovens, saw old people disturbed by the black soldiers raise their eyes to heaven, and fingered the new paper money that had replaced the *lira*. Hearing Don Gaetano made me a witness to his times. The story called the tune, and my senses – enchanted – danced behind it.

'During those months, the city let loose – parties every night, the urge to live, to start over, to make something of the aftermath. There were still bombings, this time from the Germans. They went on till spring, but we didn't pay any attention. Nobody even went to the shelters when the siren went off, so more lives were lost. Before getting out, the Germans left behind time bombs. One went off in the central post office a few days later. Total slaughter. It was one of their strategies. I heard they'd done it elsewhere too. They made poor losers.

'I was guard at an abandoned warehouse, which was still half full. A really capable fellow, all on his own and with weapons in hand, had managed to take it over and keep it from being looted. I guarded it day and night and held the insurgents' weapons. It was a good earner, but after the war money was easy. We called it *am-lire*, or American-*lire*. They printed it, but the city typographers already knew how to make it better. It was money for spending, not saving.'

'How did you get to be doorkeeper of this *palazzo*?'

'He was your father.'

Don Gaetano's answer came suddenly, and fell so hard on my ears that my nose started bleeding. I brought my hand to my face to cover it up and found it warm and wet. Don Gaetano took me to the basin to rinse off in cold water. I couldn't look him in the face.

My father. It was the first time I'd heard him mentioned, the first time I knew I'd had one.

'Sorry, Don Gaetano, but I don't feel well. Better if I go and sleep. Thank you for this day.'

I left because I needed to be alone with my thoughts.

In bed, I stuck my head under the covers. The wind was howling around the courtyard, a dog on a chain. I'd had a father, and Don Gaetano had known him. Why did I wish I hadn't heard? Why did I feel like crying? After the third 'Why?', I fell asleep. No dreams. I spent the night in a submarine, and dreams don't go that deep. Dreams are fish at the surface.

I woke up in time for school. I was bunged up in places where I'd been OK the day before. My nose and the veins all around it were purple. I said goodbye to Don Gaetano. He said he'd expect me for lunch.

My absence from school the day before was explained by my face. Visible damage earns you a bit of respect, and I'd got it by doing my duty.

I started looking at adults, considering the unlikely possibility that one of them was my father. I didn't think about my mother – Don Gaetano hadn't mentioned her, so she continued not to exist. Until the day before, my father hadn't either. But as soon as he was mentioned, he showed up in faces on the street or at school. Many were funny, some possible. It struck me for the first time that I might look like someone. I'd clear things up at lunch.

Part of me must have wondered whether Don Gaetano was my father. Now I knew the answer was no, and the news took something away without replacing it. Anna, the hiding place, the bed – they were all distant. If Don Gaetano had meant to clear them from my thoughts, he'd succeeded. And nothing about that happiness was my doing; I couldn't do a thing to bring it back. If Anna returned, she'd find me ready; if not, the happiness was over. The nerve of expectation wasn't getting wound up in my body. It's obvious that it only gets carried away when it doesn't know what to expect.

At the time, I didn't have a watch, a valuable gift my contemporaries received the day of their first communion. I'd gone through the ceremony too, but without any parents I couldn't join in with the party or refreshments afterwards. When the church bit was over, I went home.

Since I didn't have a watch, I calculated time in blocks. It was only at school that I knew what time it was. You didn't need a watch there, but everyone wore one. I didn't want one. I didn't want anything.

Most of all, the adjective 'mine' was silly. Nothing was 'mine' in the whole world, much less a father. I was using the possessive for the first time. It meant little, and only served to designate a father who hadn't been there.

That day in class, I noticed how many times the word 'father' was used: of our country, of modern physics, of the church. A lifeless word the day before, it resonated now. On my way home from school, I looked down at the ground so I wouldn't have to meet the eyes of fathers.

The absurd thing about having a father was being a son. Until yesterday, I was nobody's son, an expression I liked, since I'd read in *The Odyssey* that Nobody was Ulysses' name in Polyphemus' cave. Son of an alias, of Nobody: I liked that. It excluded everyone. But I was becoming the son of Someone, someone Don Gaetano knew, someone from the city who'd had a son at a given moment, and who knows if he'd even known about it? Now Someone was cluttering up my past. I'd become his son. As a father, one grows into a grandfather and so on. The thought was like the steps I'd groped my way up in the dark after Anna.

The fathers I saw were awful. Their kids took slaps and flying kicks. From their houses came screams, blows and sobs. None of that had happened to me. If I sometimes felt a little melancholy in the evening when mothers called their kids down in the courtyard to come back home, I remembered the beatings I could hear right down in my little room, and I came out of it even. I'd plug my ears, but it wasn't enough – I heard screams of pain from those children all the same. They are passed from one skin to another.

I'll never forget one of the kids. He was a runt like me, despite being two years older. His father was shameless about hitting him, even in the courtyard. He took the blows without a single scream, without crying. But he did move – a trembling 'No' with his head, a nervous facial tic, closing his eyes in order to endure it in front of us. I can't rid my thoughts of his image. It stays with me: a bruised saint, bleeding from the mouth. He didn't defend himself, didn't cry. He trembled with pointless heroism. He died at the hand of his father, who didn't even go to prison. Aniello, the diminutive of Gastano, his life diminished among so many whose lives were also cut short. I went to his funeral with Don Gaetano. His mother cried without tears. Aniello had played goalie for the opposing team. We were the farthest apart and exchanged glances. Whenever his father found him playing in the courtyard and wasn't happy about it, he'd yank his hair and start kicking him. Once I threw a rock at his father. He didn't even notice. We didn't matter. If someone else had thrown one at him harder, or aimed better – if we'd all thrown them at him together – we might have saved Aniello. His face, closed up so as not to give in to crying when he was hit, brought tears to my eyes. I wiped them with the back of my hand, pretending it was sweat. Without Aniello the game continued, but silently for a while.

Don Gaetano had cooked *pastepatate*, my favourite food. It looked lovely on the plate.

'You must excuse me for going off last night.'

People were walking past the lodge. Don Gaetano greeted them and out of courtesy he said, 'Want some?' Between one 'want some' and another, he fleshed out the story of what had happened before me.

My father had been a career soldier. He was forty when the war began, and he'd married my mother, who was fifteen years younger, before leaving for Africa. He came back on a leave of absence in time to find himself in civvies on Armistice Day. It was 8th September '43, the day Italy surrendered and the king fled. My father had hidden and then taken part in the uprising. He and Don Gaetano met in those days of fighting in the city. My father had single-handedly taken control of the German warehouse against a crowd who'd wanted to loot it. He planted himself in front of it in uniform, a pistol in each hand. The crowd went off to find an easier opportunity, and he installed Don Gaetano as guard. They became friends, but still used *voi* with each other.

★

It was a mad scramble after the war. The men threw themselves into making money and the women went crazy for
the Americans.

'The women of Naples lost their heads, and indeed everything else. There was an American soldier in every house.
They brought plenty – business, work. All the girls went to
their parties at Rest Camp. They'd become more beautiful and
more brazen. Public transport wasn't working so well, so the
girls asked for lifts in the Jeeps. They got picked up, and they
fell in love. There were crimes of passion. One husband
learned that his wife was going out with the Americans, but
he said nothing – it suited him. In fact, he even accompanied
her. But once his wife admitted that she enjoyed doing it with
them, he went crazy with jealousy. He killed her, his mother-
in-law, his sister-in-law and her husband. Four in one go, at
Piedigrotta.

'Naples was consumed with the tears of war. It let itself go
with the Americans, had a carnival every day. That was when I
understood the city: monarchy and anarchy. It wanted a king
but no government. It was a Spanish city. In Spain there's always
been a monarchy, as well as the strongest anarchic movement.
Naples is Spanish. It's only in Italy by mistake.

'You were barely born when your mother fell in love with an
American officer. Your father heard about it, and he came to
me. I was already working here. He'd found me the job in
his *palazzo* after having sold the contents of the warehouse to
the Americans. He came to me one morning and all he said
was: "Don Gaetano, look after the baby." He went home and
shot your mother. The same evening he boarded a ship for
America and I haven't heard anything about him since. His
name was—'

'Don't tell me, Don Gaetano. Don't put a name in my head

I'll never forget. What will I do with it? I won't use it. I've taken the name of the woman who adopted me.'

'For the first little while I looked after you.'

'So why am I learning this story today – instead of yesterday – or never?'

'Because you have to know. Yesterday you turned eighteen.'

Ah, birthdays. Another good day for other people, like Christmas and Easter. But I know when Christmas and Easter are here. You see it written all over the shops. I know my birthday is in November.

'What day was it when my mother died? Do you remember?'

'No, not the day. It was spring, in May.'

I hovered over my plate of *pastepatate*. There was a place where she was buried. I figured I'd go there with flowers. No, I'm a stranger. I don't even know her name. I would have to ask someone. No, she was gone too. They'd lived in this building. I don't want to know where. I returned to the moment after being lost in thought.

'Don Gaetano, no one makes *pastepatate* like you.'

'It's nice to see you enjoying your food. Take a bit more, there're leftovers. Go ahead.'

The widow went by wearing a brightly coloured dress. She was about to say something to me when she noticed my puffy face and turned to Don Gaetano instead, asking him to come up.

'At your service,' he replied. He hadn't dared hope.

'Will you clear up? Leave the dishes in the sink and I'll see to them later. And stay here in the lodge till I get back.'

'Not to worry.'

The son of . . . Goodbye, Nobody. Goodbye to Ulysses' forged documents. I was stuck between a murdering father and an unfaithful mother, between someone who'd fled overseas and someone who'd gone underground. I had to be like them somehow. I wasn't free to resemble Nobody. I could no longer look to the rest of the world for my origins.

Was it because of my mother that I hadn't defended myself against strangulation by Anna? Did I have her readiness to die for love? I mulled it over while I cleaned up. How did I take after my father? I wasn't jealous, either about the widow, who needed closeness, or about Anna, who wasn't for me. But I didn't have the military spirit either. To me, the boys in the uniform of the military academy seemed like convicts.

I conjured up various images in order to try to feel some jealousy: Anna writing to her boyfriend, going to see him in prison, then kissing him (who knows if you can kiss in prison?). Nope, I didn't feel a thing. How could I be jealous? She'd made that happiness with me while her boyfriend was inside. He was the one who had the right to be jealous.

Dear Father, I haven't turned out like you. I take after Don Gaetano, and you were such good friends. I learn from him every day. He's teaching me the tricks of the trade, telling me about history, and all for no reason – instead of you. Dear Father, someone's rapping on the glass. I have to see who it is. When I come back, I want you gone from my thoughts.

I dried my hands, went to the window. Anna.

'See you Sunday,' she said, and disappeared.

I felt like an idiot. I sat down in Don Gaetano's spot to look at the window and I shivered from my sacrum – they call it the *osso pezzillo* here – all the way up to my neck. A tenant went by, asked for his post, and I gave him the wrong letter. I realized it and went upstairs after him with the right one.

Then the greengrocer came by with shopping for the lady on the top floor.

As usual, he yelled up to her to let down her basket. 'Signora Sanfelice! Let down the basket, Signora Sanfelicee!'

Turning towards me: 'She doesn't hear a thing – she should wear that thing for the ears.'

'A hearing aid,' I tell him, just to say something. So he won't be talking to himself.

'That's it, an earring. Signora Sanfelicee!'

At the third yell, the lady hears, or else someone goes and knocks on her door to tell her to lower the basket.

'*Nu mumèe* – just a mo'.' Signora Sanfelice has her way, and takes her own sweet time.

Her 'moment' starts well – but never arrives. Don Gaetano says that her voice is like a toy trumpet, enough to raise the dead.

'Lower the basket!'

'Just a mo—'

'—ment,' I add, to help it along.

'The basket!' the greengrocer yells hoarsely.

'Just a mo', just a mo',' you hear coming through the open window. The lady's voice has lost all the 'ment' of moment, and for now, only 'a mo' ' drifts down.

The greengrocer loses his patience and calls up once more. While he's waiting, he says, 'That woman can't find her basket. But why doesn't she keep it near the window?'

The neighbour lady across from Signora Sanfelice yells at her to look under the sink.

The answer from the toy trumpet at full blast: 'It's not there.'

'Look behind the stove!'

'It's not there. Cuncettina's moved it. She tidies up and things disappear.'

'Signora Sanfeliceee!!!' the greengrocer tries once more, his voice strangled. What he'd really like to do is strangle her.

On cue: 'Just a mo—'

'—ment,' from me.

At last the triumphant cry comes through the courtyard. 'She's found it! She's found it!'

A voice says, 'Thy will be done,' and the window is shut. Then all the other open windows shut, one by one.

'See you Sunday.'

Had I seen her, or was it a vision? So now I've started having visions . . . St Anna is appearing to me . . . I'm only eighteen. It's not the time to start having visions. She really was here. Couldn't she have stayed a moment? No. Not a moment, or else I'd be like Signora Sanfelice with her 'Just a mo'!' It was Anna, behind the window once again. I hadn't even smelled her. I hadn't heard her voice, either. I'd read her lips: Sunday. I must have looked like a dummy.

I went to the mirror to see the face Anna had seen. Bulging eyes, mouth hanging open, skewed jaw. Unquestionably the picture of an idiot. I looked like an awestruck shepherd in a Nativity scene.

Don Gaetano returned.

'I'll make you some coffee.'

'No, I've already had some with the widow.' He was cheerful. 'You look like your father. You're thin, and your bones stick out like his. But he was all twisted nerves. His bones gave off sparks. His body churned up the air. You look like him, but you're peaceful. The chassis is like his, but there's a better engine in you.'

He was answering my thoughts. He heard them all.

'Don Gaetano, I haven't felt calm since you told me about him yesterday. Ever since I was a child, I fancied I was a part of this *palazzo*. My father was the building, my mother the courtyard. I searched every corner; that's how I knew them. It was a

version that kept me company and made a friend of the
dark. But since yesterday, I've been looking for whomever it is I
must resemble.'

Don Gaetano kept listening while he did a few things, interrupted by the tenants on their way in and out. We were used to
it and picked up where we'd left off.

'Now I'm done being a piece of this *palazzo*, because if you
take a piece away, you notice it's missing. I'm like the others – a
child who looks like a couple of people. I don't want to be a son.
I want to keep on being a piece. And if it doesn't bother you . . . I
think I resemble you. Not through heredity, but by imitation. I do
the things you teach me to do, and that's how I become like you.'

Don Gaetano passed me the work he was doing, connecting
two electrical cords so he could hang a Christmas light over
the door.

I sat down to continue. From behind, he put his hand on my
shoulder. 'You're a man now. You have to know how things
stand. You don't look like me. I grew up without any parents.
But if someone had told me who they were, I'd have hunted for
them over land and sea.'

From his pocket he pulled out a packet, long and narrow,
wrapped up in newspaper. 'It's for you. Open it.'

'A gift, Don Gaetano? For me?'

It was the first time I'd had a gift. I was still holding the cords
for the light in my hand.

'Open it.'

I quit working and felt the packet. I knew what it was. I
swallowed, my throat dry. I undid the wrapping and grasped
the bone handle of a knife. Don Gaetano took it and passed the
blade over the hair on his wrist to show me how sharp it was.
He folded the blade back into the handle, gave it back to me and
asked me to open it. The blade came out easily, without any
effort. It was sharp.

'You should carry it around with you. It's got to stay on you, got to be like your underwear: without it, you're naked. Close it up now and put it in your pocket while the tenants are going in and out.'

'It's an important gift. I owe you.'

'You owe something, but not to me. When the time comes, you'll give a knife to a young person and repay the debt that way. I got my first one from a sailor who left it lying on the ground after a brawl. I picked it up, offered it to him, and he let me have it.'

Everyone in the city had a knife in his pocket. I knew that, but I'd never felt like having one myself. Now that it was in my pocket, it was obvious that it had to stay there – because I was someone from the city, not because I was a man. Others knew when you stopped being a boy. To myself, I remained the same as before. Caught up in my thoughts, learning from everything.

'Don't use it for cutting bread or cleaning your nails. You'll use it to defend yourself. When you find yourself against the wall, unable to move back even if there's space, that's when you reach for it. Hold it low, like this, between your legs.'

He showed me the position.

'And look straight into the eyes of your enemy, who'll be blocking your path. Don't take your eyes off his.'

Don Gaetano noticed that I was looking straight at him. 'It won't happen, but that's what it's for, and only that. It's a sort of life insurance.'

I nodded and went back to the electrical cords.

The little old man from the hovel at the bottom of our alleyway came by. He knocked on the window and Don Gaetano let him in. He was dressed in rags, a patched-up jacket and a faded beret. He took it off as a gesture of respect and told Don Gaetano that his wife had been in bed for three days.

'*Nun pozzo chiamma' 'o miedeco*. I can't call the doctor. There isn't any money for it. Could this boy of yours come? He reads books.'

Don Gaetano looked at me.

'I'm studying Latin, not medicine.'

'But you're always studying and you know more than we do. We never had any schooling.'

There was nothing for it. I went with him and he wouldn't stop thanking me.

I went into the house, into the sour and smoky smell of misery. On a bench sat three women mumbling the rosary. The old lady was lying on a cot, eyes closed, lips moving mechanically. I touched her forehead: fever. I lifted the sheet. There was the smell of sores, ulcers beginning on her heels.

'*Piaghe da decubito*. Bed sores,' I said quietly.

Behind me, one of the three women asked what I'd said.

'*La paga di subbito*. Pay him right away!'

'Oh, *mamma mia*,' said one of them in reply.

'Young man, we'll pay you eight days from now.'

'So what is he, some pizza guy you pay eight days later?'

I told the old man that ointment and bandages were needed and I went to the chemist. I was glad to have a bit of money in my pocket. I bought what I needed on the advice of the chemist, along with tablets for the fever.

I went back and tended the sores, which were just starting up. The tablet was difficult. She'd never swallowed one before. I went to the baker and he gave me a slice of bread. I made a little ball out of the doughy part with the pill inside. She took it like that.

The rosary continued, happy to have procured an intervention. The little old man wanted to kiss my hand and I kept pulling it back. I told him to continue giving her the tablets and left.

Don Gaetano was settling a quarrel between two tenants. One was complaining that the other one upstairs was hanging her laundry out to dry and it was dripping over her own, which was nearly dry. It was a simple matter, but they had to scream until the whole *palazzo* knew about it. Don Gaetano listened to the two angry voices, ready to tear each other's hair out.

They'd started arguing on their balconies and he'd invited them to continue in the lodge. I got there when they were well into it and already hoarse. I sat down at the table to continue connecting the wires. There were often quarrels – sticky ones – since there were so many of us all on top of each other. We wore each other down. They're called 'sticky' because they contain an adhesive that gets mixed in with the words and sends them to the hands – and then you need a solvent to pry them apart. Don Gaetano used to say, 'Donkeys get stuck and spill their carts.' For the 'stickies' between women, he had a solvent that worked like magic: he'd offer them a cup of coffee.

They made peace. Don Gaetano's coffee had judiciary powers. It was a court of appeal that always settled rows. As my contribution to the successful outcome, I turned on the Christmas lights. The two women embraced and left arm in arm, confiding in each other.

'Don Gaetano, what do you put in the coffee to get that effect?'

' *'A pacienza*, I throw in a bit of patience. It's a root that grows in our alleyways. Those two needed to let off steam, get out of the house. They needed someone to sit and listen to them.'

★

The days of the week went by. December was already here, and the tip of the volcano was dressed in snow. At night, the *tramontana* made ice on the ground; by day, crystals in the sky.

'It's like a lid of turquoise.' A second-floor tenant, the pensioner Professor Cotico, devoted himself to poetry. He'd compose it, then come through the lodge reciting the verses he'd just written. The *tramontana* inspired him.

'A morning so cold, it could split your nails.'

'*Prufesso*', someone's already written that and set it to music. Those verses are by Ernesto Murolo.'

'Is that so? One can hardly write a line here before someone pops up and says: "I got there first." But gentlemen, poetry isn't a tram on which the first to board sits down and the others stand up. Poetry isn't a race where someone has to come first. Every day is born innocent of poetry. Someone wakes up and renews it.'

'Well, yes – the first to wake rewrites *The Divine Comedy*.'

'Don Gaetano, you're too harsh a critic. Listen to this other verse:

'e pure a mezzogiorno
'o friddo s'accaniva senza scuorno.

and the cold at midday
remained, shameless.'

'That one's yours, Professor. No one is going to take it from you. You can copyright it.'

'About time!'

That autumn I got to know the tenants. From inside the lodge, you'd see them going by, one at a time, and they assumed types. The lodge window was like a magnifying glass for stamps. The tenants were less interesting than the characters I read about in Don Raimondo's books, but more individual. Each one had adopted a bearing to distinguish himself from the others and so as not to get lost among so many of us. There was a competition between faces for the most unusual look, and it was the same with their voices, greetings and habits. They obeyed only one law – be different, stand out from one another – and they applied it rigorously. If one person had a canary on the balcony, the next-door neighbour would keep a goldfinch, and the person on the floor below would get a crossbreed. One comfortably-off woman kept three medium-sized dogs and she'd take them out for walks on three long leads that got tangled around everything she met in the street. The old man from the hovel, the one who'd come about his sick wife, used to set his chair outside his door to have a smoke. As if on cue, the dogs on their leads would surround him, and they'd end up tethered around his chair, moving it around and threatening to topple it. Then the *signora* would untangle their leads and continue her tumultuous descent, the voice of her neighbour opposite trailing behind:

'There goes the *signora*, out hunting again this morning!'

Cummoglio, the accountant, is unlucky in business. He comes from a family of button manufacturers – *buttunari* – who were ruined by the arrival of the zipper. Before the war, he started selling wooden ice-chests, but he had to stop because of competition from refrigerators. He stoically moved into woollen mattresses just when sprung ones started coming in.

Don Gaetano always said of him that if he threw straw into water it would sink, while someone else could throw in lead and it would float. His wife, Signora Euterpe, had given birth to twins. They were my age, and named Oreste and Pilade, after the inseparable pair from Greek mythology. They were so alike that not even their parents could tell them apart. They got the same haircut on purpose, so that everyone would confuse them, and even knotted their ties the same way; if one of them got hurt, the other one stuck on a plaster as well. They'd break out laughing at the same time. They rigorously applied themselves to looking exactly the same, and took advantage of it, changing names and places. They themselves must have believed that they were simultaneously one and the other. They took care over being doubles.

Cummoglio had abandoned the attempt to tell them apart and never called them by name. He'd given them a collective nickname, *I Vuie*, You Two. They willingly responded to it. If he wanted only one of them, he'd call out 'One of You Two!' The rest of us called them *I Vuie* too.

That school year I noticed a difference between them. One of them couldn't say the Neapolitan 'sh' for 's' very well, as in *shcuola*, school, *shchifo*, disgusting, or *shfizio*, fantasy. He had to hesitate, and said *sh-cuola*, struggling over the 'sh'. To cover up for him, the other one faked the same difficulty. But sometimes he'd forget, and that's how I noticed. I'd decided it was Pilade who could say the 'sh' and Oreste who couldn't. *'O rest'* means 'the rest' in Neapolitan. And Oreste was missing the rest of their likeness.

That autumn in class, I began using their names without getting mixed up. They were dismayed, and feared losing their doubleness. They pulled me aside and asked me how I could tell them apart. I said I'd never tell anyone how, not even them.

'You keep the secret of your name, and I'll keep the secret of the game.'

The joke hit home. I was a reserved kid. Secrets and hiding places were safe with me.

'We believe you,' said one of the two. He instinctively used the pronoun 'we'. I never had any occasion to use it, and I liked hearing them say it.

From that moment on, I was a danger to them. They avoided me, and if I called one of them by name, neither responded.

It was Sunday before I knew it. It went by – and Anna didn't come. I stayed in the lodge that afternoon, finishing a second Christmas light to put above the glass there. Don Gaetano went out for a walk. The courtyard was full of glistening light burnished by the frosty *tramontana*.

The sun beat against the glass in the windows of the upper floors and relayed splashes of light back down to the ground. The windows in Naples passed the sun between them. Those who had more because of their position gave it to those down below, who had less. They made a good team. The glaziers actually put them in a bit askew in order to multiply the reflective surfaces. A cannon of light arrived down in the lodge after bouncing off ten other windows before it got to the little hole I sat in.

Don Gaetano says it's a good sign. The sun loves those who live way down low, where it doesn't arrive. It loves the blind more than anyone else, and has a special caress for their eyelids. It doesn't like its worshippers, who lie nude under its abundance and use it to colour their skin. The sun wants to warm people without coats, whose teeth chatter in the narrow alleyways. It calls them outside, getting them to leave their cold little rooms, and then rubs them till they smile at its tickling.

'It's a good sign. It loves you and is sending its greeting to you inside the *stanzino*. The windows are its steps, and its light descends them out of affection for you. It means the sun is protecting you.'

I didn't wait in the street for Anna. If she knocked on the door, I'd hear her. I felt for my knife. The handle was bone, light-coloured.

I touched the blade to my cheek to test the edge. I remembered Don Gaetano's advice, to keep it for protection, and not use it for anything else. You couldn't take liberties with a knife. It was a serious tool. If you treated it with respect, it would do its duty when necessary. But if you played around with it and showed it off, it would slip from your hand just when you needed it.

The knife and men from the south went together.

I didn't let myself think about how to use it at a dangerous moment. I'd improvise. You don't ponder an act of violence. It's violent to throw yourself between feet to grab a ball with your hands. The kick to my nose wasn't the act of violence, it was diving between all those feet. If I'd thought about it first, I wouldn't have done it.

That's how it will be with the knife. If I get into a tight spot, I'll find the defensive move I need.

Don Gaetano returned and we started putting up the Christmas lights. On the door, above the window of the lodge, the blinking lights winked at the holiday. This was how Don Gaetano got out of celebrating every year. He never put up a Nativity scene.

'People who have children do it to make them fond of the Bible story.'

We didn't have families, and we weren't a family.

Those with some social standing used Christmas to show off. Hampers brimming with things to eat would arrive for them in the lodge. Even those who had nothing ran up debts to make an impression. La Capa took his family to the theatre in a taxi, and then came to tell us about it. His wife, short and squat, went out all gussied up, but with a curtain around her and a lampshade on her head, she still looked like a barrel. She called the taxi driver 'chauffeur'. La Capa was part mortified, part proud, which is why he told Don Gaetano everything.

'The other evening they performed *False Daft* at San Carlo.'

'What do you mean, *False Daft*? Which was it, False or Daft?'

'Don Gaetano, the opera: *False Daft*.'

'But what do you mean *False Daft*? Was it really silly?'

'No. *False Daft*. That's it.'

'But what are you going on about? Did you laugh?'

Don Gaetano was scared of La Capa, but he wouldn't let him get away with it. La Capa couldn't say *Falstaff*.

'Don Gaetano, I'm surprised that with all your education, you don't know the opera by maestro Ver— Ver— What's his name?'

'*Verme*? Worm?'

'Ver— Ver— I can't seem to remember the name of that maestro.'

'*Verza*. Cabbage.'

'No, it wasn't Cabbage. In fact the crème de la crème were there – the magistrate, the chief constable, the mayor with all the town's other finery.'

'Ah, so he wanted to wear it.'

'What?'

'His finery.'

'What finery! Don Gaetano, you're confusing me with these details.'

With La Capa, it was impossible to get to the end of a story. You just gave up.

The latest was that his wife had made him get a *barboncino*, a poodle, 'Because it's chic,' she told him. So they brought home a white one. La Capa had consulted Don Gaetano.

'What do you say, Don Gaetano? Are we doing the right good thing, taking this dog? It's a Bourbon.'

'So you should call it Ferdinando.'[6]

6 Ferdinando was the name of several of the Bourbon kings of Naples.

'Would you say so?'

'Bourbon dogs have absolutely got to be called Ferdinando. If they're Savoy dogs, then you have to call them Umberto.'[7]

'Well, no. It's pure-bred Bourbon.'

I asked Don Gaetano how someone as serious and hardworking as La Capa could willingly expose himself to ridicule, practically ask for it. This guy who'd known the depths of misery and now had some comforts was ruining it all by insisting on passing for a gentleman.

'When a poor person gets money, the first thing he does is buy himself something to wear. He puts on a good fabric and thinks he's someone else. But that's all money can do – make you *seem*. La Capa wants to seem like someone else and so he trips up. When he knelt down to measure shoes, nobody laughed at him. They say money doesn't smell. But actually it does, and it makes the people who wear it smell too.'

The beginning of the month sees visits from Signorina Scafarèa. She's habitually late with the rent. Every day she shows up: 'Has the money order come yet?' She waits for a transfer from her brother in America, and gets by on that. She pays the rent with half of it and with the rest she struggles on for the month. She's shrivelled like a prune and her garlicky breath would slay a fly. She never finds the window of the lodge open without sticking her head in, asking a question and leaving her mark on the air. If she comes by at lunchtime, she can take away your appetite. When the money order comes, Don Gaetano rushes out to take it to her.

I saw Anna again as I was leaving school. She was sitting in the café opposite with the bleached blonde. It was the kind of day when lizards slither out from under rocks to bask in the sun.

7 The House of Savoy ruled the united Kingdom of Italy from 1861 until the end of the Second World War. Umberto II was the last king.

After the *tramontana*'s slaps, the *scirocco* brought caresses. The cafés had put up tables outside.

She waved and invited me to come over. I was ashamed to stand in front of them, a schoolboy with books under his arm.

'I'm thinking of renting that apartment. One of these days I'll come and take some measurements. Will you help me?'

'If the need arises.' I stayed frozen to the spot and didn't say anything else. Embarrassed, I said goodbye. Behind my back I heard the other one go, 'If the need arises' and laugh. Fair enough. How had I managed to come out with that? I hadn't expected to see Anna, and even less to hear the formal *lei* from her. 'She' from her: the words seemed silly even to me and I smiled at myself. Some days one is bound to be ridiculous, even without La Capa's money. With those two in the café, I hadn't been able to muster the bit of seriousness I had in the lodge. Probably I was ridiculous there too, without realizing it.

That meeting hadn't happened by chance. Anna must have found me, chosen the spot and faked her surprise. Was she trying to reassure me that she'd come back? I asked in my heart, and I heard Anna's thoughts telling me 'Yes'.

I ran into a man standing still.

'Watch your manners, young man.'

'Excuse me. Please pardon me. I didn't see you.'

'Well then, I must have become invisible!'

Inside me I heard Anna laughing.

Why did she have to fake it? Was someone watching her? Was that girl checking up on her? There was no answer.

Was I able to hear people's thoughts, like Don Gaetano? I'd had one from Anna and she'd got mine, too. I tried again. Nothing. The line was dead.

Sometimes you try something and it works, but you don't

know why and you can't do it again. With me, things happened by mistake. I'd try to reconstruct the situation. How did I feel the day before happiness? How was I five minutes before I asked Anna for confirmation and bumped into someone? I'd already forgotten, and I couldn't do it again.

Don Gaetano was sitting at the table by the time I got back to the lodge.

'Don Gaetano, I've brought you some *baccalà* all soaked and spongy, just how you like it.'

'You shouldn't have. I could smell as soon as you came in the door that you had *baccalà* with you. Come and sit down.'

'And I could smell from the door that you'd cooked *pastepatate*. Yum!'

I washed my hands, which were seasoned with *baccalà*, and from the bathroom I said I'd seen Anna. 'She says she wants to come and live here.'

'It's not true.'

'What does she want, then, according to you?'

Don Gaetano let me sit down and start taking my first bites. 'Anna wants to see blood.'

I couldn't wait, and asked with my mouth full, 'And what will she do when she sees it?'

Don Gaetano took a sip of wine to clean his mouth. 'Blood is truth. It doesn't tell lies when it comes out and it doesn't go back. That's how words must be as well. After you say them, you can't take them back. Anna wants to see the truth come out.'

He spoke quietly. He was saying something simple, but I didn't understand it. I preferred to keep my mouth shut over the *pastepatate*. It was clear that happiness was truth and was paid for in blood.

'Anna will be back,' I said, meaning that I couldn't do anything about it.

Don Gaetano nodded. I wiped my bowl clean with some bread.

'She looked pretty, waiting outside the school. She was wearing nylon stockings, and the sun was playing with her hair. She's interested in me because I'm the most ordinary of all the tenants, someone who doesn't matter very much.'

'Don't put yourself down with anyone. You're good stuff, and you'll make something of yourself.'

Don Gaetano kept me going.

'Anyone who grows up by himself in a *stanzino* and instinctively behaves well has something special to offer. You have to defend it, even if it seeps out with your blood.'

That didn't make me squeamish. Before Anna, I thought it was good for blood to churn around in your body in the dark. It couldn't gain anything by coming out and drying up in the light; outside the body it didn't have a function. Now I knew that it would help Anna, and perhaps she'd get better if someone let his own blood in front of her. I knew I was ready, and it didn't matter when. *Sì*: Anna's voice reached me once more. Then, *Yes*, I promise I'll obey that *sì*. I'll say 'Yes' more often than 'no', and more yeses than noes will govern my actions. Even if I must say 'No', it will be at the service of 'Yes'. Will I spare my blood before Anna? *No*.

'Her boyfriend, a *camorrista*, is coming out of prison. They're letting him out around Christmas.'

'I heard she had a boyfriend. I'm happy for Anna that he's free.'

Don Gaetano started clearing things. I did the washing up.

'Someone has to go and see the widow. Do you want to go up?'

'Did she ask you to go?'

'Don't ask questions when it comes to women. Do you want to go?'

Warmth travelled from my stomach to just a bit lower. 'OK.'

*

The months of heated embraces were over. Anna's wanting me was over too. She'd sucked the fruit and spat out the stone. I looked in the mirror for changes. My face was the same – long, easily bewildered, with faraway eyes. My nose was even more swollen, the skin dark purple over my cheekbones. My body was more defined, my ribs visible as well as the contours of my chest, and small, rounded muscles rippled over my stomach.

I went up to the widow's. She had heating in her flat, and opened the door to me in her dressing-gown. She took my hand and I followed her into her room. I felt increasing urgency and embraced her forcefully. I pushed her against the wall instead of the bed, and thrust into her standing up, still in my clothes. Rather than letting her make all the moves, I made up some of my own on the spot. I was taller and she clung to me, lifting first one leg and then the other. Suddenly she was in my arms, her legs wrapped around my back. I held her like that until I came. I pulled her away from the wall and laid her down on the bed. She smoothed my damp hair, kissed me all over my face. Then she made some coffee and wanted to serve it to me in bed. She'd never been so attentive before. I saw her smile for the first time when she came in with the tray. Our embraces were silent. Her smile made up for the missing words. I drank the coffee, her thank-you to me. She saw me to the door and put my toolbox on my shoulders.

The door closed only after I got down to the first landing.

Something had happened to make me different. The world's respect comes suddenly, and you don't know it's coming or how to explain it.

Something had happened in the lodge too. The window had been broken. Don Gaetano had called the expert glazier who was measuring it up. I didn't ask. There were strangers about. Professore Cotico ruled: 'Broken window and doorkeeper, 27 and 68, lucky numbers.' Don Gaetano left me in charge of the lodge and went with the glazier. The passing tenants greeted me as they did Don Gaetano. The count came by: 'Young man, you owe me a rematch. Don't forget!' He'd used the formal *voi* with me. I was stunned. I felt drained, as if I needed sleep.

After an hour the glazier came back without Don Gaetano. I helped him install the new glass and secure it with sealant. It was a bit crooked.

Don Gaetano found the work done and the lodge in order. I asked what had happened.

'Didn't you hear anything when you were up with the widow?'

'Not a thing.'

'Anna's boyfriend came round looking for you. He acted the thug, flipped the table over. Wanted to know where you were. People stopped and stared. He threw a punch at the window with a gloved hand. Someone started screaming "Police!" and he went off. He says he'll be back and he'll leave you wherever he finds you.'

'And did he do anything to you? Did he put a hand on you? Did he insult you?' I said it loudly, which surprised me. I was angry with the guy who'd threatened Don Gaetano instead of me.

'He didn't do anything to me, just those stunts with the table and the window.'

That's why people had changed towards me from one minute to the next. Word had spread. Don Gaetano asked me what I wanted to do.

'Nothing. If Anna wants to find me, I'm here, and the same goes for him.' The words came out by themselves, as if deciding for me. Having said them, I couldn't take them back. Hearing them, I knew they were right. Was this the blood Anna needed? The blood of two young men pitted against each other? It was

Erri De Luca

what Don Gaetano had warned me about, but you only understand something when it happens to you.

I smiled at Don Gaetano in thanks for the knife. He nodded. It was a serious acknowledgement, and he was somewhat embarrassed.

'It won't be today,' he said. 'Let's do what we need to do. I'll cook potatoes, onions and tomatoes and we'll put the *baccalà* into that. And we'll have our game of *scopa*.'

Don Gaetano left me alone. I saw everything around me clearly. Outside was the early darkness of December. The sealant around the newly fitted window smelled of wax and rubber. The *baccalà* steamed away tastily. Thoughts were so many clothes hung out to dry. The *scopa* cards suggested to me the order in which to play them. I guessed which ones Don Gaetano held in his hand. Or maybe he told me.

'Don Gaetano, can you transmit your own thoughts to someone else?'

'No, I receive them. That's it.'

'Don Gaetano, you're distracted tonight. I don't recognize you. You've let me sweep seven and I have the *settebello*.'

'I had to. I'm not distracted. You're the one who's playing like a dream tonight. I'm not sure I can win.'

'That broken glass and the nasty visit have put you in a bad mood.'

'I'm the same player every evening, but you've changed and you haven't noticed.'

I hadn't noticed it. I wasn't even surprised to win two games running. Nothing seemed different from usual, when I lost. I got up to turn over the *baccalà* with the other stuff in the saucepan. Someone was knocking at the window. Don Gaetano got up suddenly and went to the door. Instead of letting the person in, he went out himself. I watched them from my side of the

100

glass while I tasted the cooking. I couldn't see their faces. The man was dressed elegantly in a nice light coat, and he was gesturing with his hands. Don Gaetano kept his behind his back, leaning forward slightly to listen. The man made a gesture that ended the conversation. He put his hand to his wallet, but Don Gaetano stopped his arm. The man insisted on giving him money; he had to take it. The man pressed it into his hand. It had to be money for the new window. The man put a hand on Don Gaetano's shoulder and they embraced.

Don Gaetano came back in and I looked up at him as if to ask what had happened. He left the money on the table.

'The toss of a coin is about to determine the value of your life. A broken glass is paid for and the local boss says: "I can't do a thing about it. *O bbrito se pava, l'annore no e se lava"*.'

'*O bbrito*: It was a long time since I'd heard the word 'glass' in dialect. A window could be paid for; honour, no. Dialect was particularly good for judgement, better than the Latin mass.

'Did you ask for his help, Don Gaetano? Let it go. We'll handle it ourselves and hopefully no one will get hurt. Don't give it another thought.'

He nodded in defeat.

That evening we relished a *baccalà* fit for kings, drank wine and Don Gaetano told me war stories that opened my ears and tugged at my heartstrings.

The Germans had mined the aqueduct to blow it sky-high. A group of them were taken prisoner by the Neapolitans, and to save their lives they said they knew where the bombs were. Don Gaetano and some others were ordered to go with the prisoners to deactivate them.

The Neapolitans had taken guns from the barracks. If they were asked nicely, the *carabinieri* sometimes distributed their share out of loyalty to the king. But in other barracks, requests for more guns were turned away for fear of a German reprisal. So the people came back with a bit more force to requisition them. There was a second front; the Fascists shot at the crowd of insurgents from the houses. There were skirmishes on the stairs of *palazzi*, on the rooftops, on-the-spot executions. One of our men was captured by the Germans and put against a wall, but at that very moment a German officer arrives followed by our lot, and he uses the guy on the wall as a shield. So the Germans are trying to open up an escape route but they're surrounded on all sides and attacked. Our own man, really brave, is saved. His name was Schettini, and Don Gaetano knew him.

I listened to the stories about the city and recognized it as my own. Don Gaetano gave me his own citizenship in small doses. It was the story of the many clinging together to become a people, a story that had been forgotten in a hurry. It was good, like the *baccalà* in the saucepan. There are moments of greatness when you hurl yourself against barriers in waves like the southwest wind, which lasts for three days and cleans the air in your lungs.

'In via Foria the tram barricades blocked the Panzer tanks for hours. Eventually they managed to get through, but not to via Roma. Men and boys came down on the attack from the alleyways on the hill and launched bombs and gunfire at the caterpillars. The armoured cars couldn't do a thing against these these wild hoards, and they retreated.'

I asked how a revolt begins.

'The first day's attack was against a German lorry that had gone to plunder a shoe factory. At the end of September, the Germans had begun looting whatever they could from shops, even from churches. It started with an unplanned assault on one of their lorries loaded with shoes, that first battle.'

American ships were in sight and the Germans were about to leave. So why risk it when we were so close to liberation? In Rome, months later and under the same conditions, nothing had happened. The people had waited.

'The retreat wasn't definite. They had enough troops to fight back. They'd prepared their defence against the landing in the city, and were getting ready to fight. Everyone's anger had intensified. The men who were hiding were pressing to come up from under the tufa. There was a forced evacuation from the coastal region. People living within 300 metres of the coast had to leave their homes. This city is right next to the sea, and vacating those 300 metres from one day to the next created 100,000 evacuees, just camping out, with no idea where they should go.

'So yes, we could have waited too, put our heads down and counted the minutes. And I don't know why we all leapt into the street like crickets. What goads you into action at times like those is partly personal, and partly to do with that group we call "a people". People around you are doing what you're doing, and you're doing what they're doing. One minute you're ahead of everyone, and then they overtake you. Someone falls over dead beside you, and the rest continue what was started in his or her name. It's like music. Everyone plays his instrument and what comes out is not the sum total of the players but the music, a current that moves in waves and skims the sea. It's a hunger that allows you to see bread that's been thrown away and leave it for someone else, a mother handing her child a stone to throw, a shared emotion that makes you see blood, not tears. I can't explain it to you, that uprising. If you find yourself caught up in one, you'll take part in it and it won't be like the one I'm telling you about. And yet it will be the same, because all people's revolts against armed forces are related.'

★

I understood the uprising in fits and starts, and I imagined it jerkily too, like the resurrection of a body: first, a nervous contraction, then, like a tic, a muscle in the finger moves, an awakening that begins at the edges of the body. Only after he sat up did Lazarus remember having heard the voice commanding him to come forth. That's how I imagined the uprising: as a rush of energy in a lifeless body. But how had it shut down? How had it ended up as a tin soldier?

At school I could never have heard a lesson as accurate as Don Gaetano's story. There we studied up to the First World War, and then the school year ended along with the 1900s. A young man had shot an archduke and the world had gone to war with itself, divided between those who sided with the archduke and those with the young man. Italy sided at first with the archduke and kept quiet about it, then went over to the side of the young man. The First World War was one long trench, a place where man already has one foot in the grave. But the Second World War, was it a relapse? I couldn't imagine the youths who'd been melted into tin soldiers. They'd turned into the adults around me, and their decimated generation was the most troubled in the history of the world.

'I knew a lad who was twenty at the start of the war. He was honest, studious, poor and well intentioned. To get by, he gave private lessons to students. He fell in love with a girl and used to go to her house to teach her Italian and maths. The romance came to light only later. His father had died, and he wore strict mourning: a black jacket shiny with wear that had holes in the elbows. He was in love, and it upset him that he couldn't wear a little colour. He was passionate about his subjects and knew much of Dante's poetry by heart. In June of '40, Italy joins the war and he signs up as a volunteer. Doesn't wait to be called up, doesn't take advantage of being his mother's sole support, willingly signs up with the Navy. Finally he can doff the mourning, delighted to be able to show up in the blue uniform of the Navy officer. He made long, patriotic speeches, but his real enthusiasm was for the colourful uniform he wore. He appeared in it to give his final lessons. The girl, who learned later how much he loved her, wrote essays, which he saved. It was his mother, the widow, who told her when the girl went to visit her.

'In a nutshell, he makes it in time to embark and to die in the naval conflict offshore of Teulada in November '40. He had a beautiful face – dark, serious and eager – and his blue uniform became the clothes of a youth he'd missed out on.

'That's how one gets thrown into the war. And don't go thinking it's small beer.'

'I won't, Don Gaetano. I'd do it for Anna.'

At the end of the uprising, the first American Jeep drove along the shore, preceded by one of our soldiers in bersagliere uniform, crying out: 'It's over! We've won!' The Germans were still at Capodimonte with their heavy artillery to cover the retreat.

The black market got going immediately with American stuff off the ships. All that abundance disappeared by the truckload from the warehouses. People even carried things away through the sewers. Don Gaetano saw a manhole pop up in the middle of Santa Lucia, and a head stick out to look around. He went over to lend a hand and help the guy out, but heard only: 'Excuse me – wrong street.' And the guy slid down again, closing the manhole behind him.

That evening lasted longer than the others. Don Gaetano was handing over a history. It was a legacy. His stories were becoming my memories. I understood where I'd come from. I wasn't the son of the *palazzo*, but of the city. I wasn't an orphan. I was part of a people.

We parted company at midnight. I got up from the chair, having grown. I was taller, and under my feet was a foundation that gave me a few new centimetres. He'd instilled in me a sense of belonging. I was from Naples, with all the compassion, anger and also the shame of someone who is born late.

In my little room, I thought about that other day before, the Saturday with Anna. This day before was better. It held growth, the unanticipated respect of the people around me, coffee with the widow, games won at *scopa*. This day before held more promise. Was I downgrading Anna? No. She came before everything. The days before and the days after all hinged on her. My 'yes' to everything came from her.

I slept soundly. As soon as I awoke, my first move was for the knife. I thought: it's not for now.

Don Gaetano was upstairs, cleaning. I left him a note. In the alleyway someone touched his hat in greeting.

At school, I listened closely to the lessons. I realized the importance of the things I was learning. It was wonderful that a man presented them to a group of seated boys, that they listened enthusiastically and grasped them straightaway. Wonderful, a room you could be in to learn. Wonderful, the oxygen that attached itself to blood and carried both blood and words to the edges of the body. Wonderful, the names of the moons surrounding Jupiter, wonderful, the Greeks' cry 'The sea! The sea!' as they retreated. Wonderful, Xenophon's having written it down so it wouldn't be forgotten. Wonderful, too, Pliny's account of the eruption of Vesuvius. Their writing absorbed the tragedies, transformed them into narrative in order to transmit them and so overcome them. Light entered your mind just like it did the classroom. Outside it was sparkling, a May day shuffled into the deck of December.

I headed for home, still thinking about the lessons. There was a civic generosity in the state schools, which were free and allowed someone like me to learn. I had grown up within it and wasn't aware of the effort it took for society to fulfil its obligations. Education made something of us poor people. The rich would be taught anyway. School gave weight to those who had nothing and evened things out. It didn't abolish misery, but within its walls it made us equals. Disparity began outside.

I went by Don Raimondo's to return a book of Neapolitan poetry by Salvatore Di Giacomo: our favourite.

'It's never been as beautiful as this, our dialect.'

'You're right, Don Raimondo. I really liked the sheet that came down from heaven to earth and gathered up a crowd of poor people to eat in heaven. Don Gaetano's *pastepatate* tastes a bit like that manna.'

Don Raimondo enjoyed chatting a bit about the books he lent me. That day, for the first time, I didn't ask for one to take away. He was astonished.

'I have an exam. I'll take up reading again later.' I didn't know whether I'd be able to bring it back to him.

I walked light-heartedly on my way home from school, which was in an open space near the sea. At the entrance to the alleyway I saw the little old man coming towards me, the one for whom I'd been a fake doctor. He seized my hand and I shook his, just in case he started all over again trying to kiss mine in gratitude.

'*Nun ce iate.* Don't go there – he's waiting for you.' He held me back and urged me to turn around. Even if I hadn't had my back to the wall, for me there was no getting out of this. I had to go to my post. I asked him how his wife was and he let go of my hands to take off his hat in thanks. 'She's well, thanks to you.' I took advantage of his answer to free myself and go on my way. His words came after me.

'For the love of Jesus Christ, don't go there! Don't go.'

★

No one else greeted me along the alleyway climbing the hill. I went through the door. Anna. I immediately saw Anna in front of the lodge window.

'I'm waiting for you.' The voice from the courtyard was trying to sound tough.

'I'm not,' I said to myself more than to him. 'I don't need to wait.'

I watched Anna while the footsteps came towards me. I smiled at her shiny, *marron glacé* hair.

'I'm waiting for you.' The voice from the courtyard was louder this time. There was no one besides us three, no noise. The lodge was empty. I put my books down on the ground in front of it. Anna looked at me, her eyes staring, her mouth slightly open. If she was crazy, it was the raw nerve of her beauty.

'Here I am, Anna,' I said as I passed her.

I liked the emptiness around us. No distractions. It was just us. Full stop.

'So, piece of shit, are you gonna come 'ere, or do I have to come an' take you by the ears?'

I figured he needed the whole place to hear him, not me. Outside school, the kids would bawl out threats they'd picked up in the street, saying I'll do this to you and Fine then, I'll do that. I didn't care for all this shouting and bullying. Head down, I entered the courtyard.

The voice was in the middle. I hadn't yet looked up.

I saw his shoes first, shiny and new. La Capa would have appreciated them. Then his neatly pressed trousers, then the rest. He was dressed in his Sunday best: double-breasted blazer, tie, even a flower in his buttonhole. Handsome face. Black moustache, brilliantined hair. Anna had chosen someone with presence. He kept his eyes narrowed. I looked up at the May sky at Christmas-time for a second, then fixed my eyes on his and didn't take them off him.

He held a knife in his hand, and he was picking at his nails with it. I took a few steps towards him and noticed that I was taller. The sun didn't reach the ground. It was ricocheting between the windows, bouncing the light around. It occurred to me that it would protect me, just as Don Gaetano had said.

I didn't notice that Anna had entered the courtyard behind me. While I took the knife out of my jacket, a thought came to me and I held on to it.

'*Si' muorto, piezz'e mmerda.* You're dead, you piece of shit,' he said as he came forward. I held the knife low between my legs and in front of my groin, pointed down to the ground. He held his in his right hand. I held mine in my left.

He made a short lunge, then one a bit longer, and I took a step to the side and one backwards. I wasn't moving in to attack. I had to defend myself. The attack was up to him. I noticed Anna, because between us there was a third breath deeper than ours. Each time he lunged, I moved to the side, always clockwise. I was trying to circle the courtyard. He grew impatient and went straight for me, shouting. Our knives met, injuring my right arm and grazing his ribs. It was goodbye to his jacket. The first blood ruined it, along with his waistcoat. My sleeve, light grey, was ripped, with a dark stain I saw only later.

Anna let out a hoarse scream. He looked at his jacket. I took the opportunity to move to another spot in the courtyard.

A woman yelled, '*Fermateli, s'accidono*! Stop them! They'll kill each other!'

The sound of windows opening. No more spying in silence: blood had been spilled.

At the sight of his ruined clothes, he became enraged by the insult and lurched around, shouting, 'Now you're dead!'

He came towards me, arms spread for hand-to-hand combat.

I raised myself up to my full height. He lifted his head to look me in the face. As I'd hoped, he was struck by the light bouncing off the windows. While he was temporarily blinded by the sun's reflections, I seized the opportunity to make my single lunge with the knife. It went through his side near the liver.

He stopped immediately, threw down his weapon, put his hand to his side and crumpled to his knees. Anna broke into sobs and started weeping.

I put the knife down on the ground. It wasn't going to help with anything else. Standing between us, her face contorted by grief, Anna wept. I saw by the light of the courtyard that she was covered in bruises.

People started coming in. Don Gaetano took me by the arm and led me away. I picked up the books in front of the lodge. My right arm was bleeding profusely. People moved apart for us as we walked through the crowd. Half the *palazzo* was there. Some said, 'You did the right thing,' while others cried, 'Murderer!' Even *I Vuie*, the twins, were there, and I heard, 'Let's *sh-cram!*' It was Oreste.

No one tried to stop me while I walked arm in arm with Don Gaetano. At the entrance, I recognized the light-coloured coat from the previous evening. I let myself be led away. Blood was draining from me and I was fading with it. Don Gaetano put his coat over my arm to hide the injury. As we carried on down the alleyway, we passed a couple of policemen going up.

We went into a chemist's. The doctor took us in the back and stopped the blood. He stitched up the cut really well. They said nothing to each other, or to me. We left after buying more bandages.

★

I went down to the marina at Don Gaetano's side. Nature had embraced the entire city that day. At Santa Lucia, tourists and the coachmen in their horse-drawn carriages rolled up their sleeves. We carried on. I didn't ask questions. The sun was absorbent. It dried my blood, the paint on the boats and the misery of people who'd come down out of the cold alleyways to enjoy its heat. Spread out along the pavement – better than at home in bed – they asked for charity, smiling gratefully for the warmth.

The carriages took American soldiers around, the descendants of those who'd arrived in the liberated city. Why were they still here? Because they were the heirs of that victory. Can you inherit victory? It should last as long as the enemy's on the ground, and then stop.

For me it was hardly a matter of victory. I'd only saved myself with the knife. Now I was going away, whereas winners stay, like the Americans.

Where was Don Gaetano taking me? Certainly not to the police. Maybe it was my turn to find a hiding place. The one beneath the lodge was out. Anna knew about it.

I felt feverishly tired at the sight of this excessive beauty. 'This is my city, Don Gaetano.'

'Say goodbye to it. Tonight you're leaving for America. You've got a ticket under another name on a ship headed for Argentina. I'll give you your papers later.'

'You knew.'

What was life made of, if you could foresee every detail? Foresee, but be unable to intervene or prevent things happening? This was Don Gaetano's habitual sadness. His only remedies were solutions after the event: a ticket for America, the same trip he'd made. The ocean was an escape route for us southerners. It gave us absolution, something impossible on earth. My thoughts were churning chaotically in my head. Don Gaetano was listening.

'The sea will settle our accounts.'

It occurred to me to ask, 'Are you coming too?'

'No, I'm staying. I'll cover your back. When it's safe for you to return, I'll let you know. You're going to stay with a friend. He'll come to collect you when you get off the boat.'

Return? I don't think I'll be coming back to a place where blood's been shed. I won't go back up the streets I've come down.

'If I had a father, he wouldn't be doing this for me.'

'We don't know that. You and I didn't have one, and we don't understand it.'

We sat down on a bench facing the sea.

'You're weak. You've lost blood.'

'I had more than I needed. I had enough for her. It managed to make her shed tears. They're precious, Don Gaetano, Anna's tears. They're the way out of her craziness. It wasn't our blood she wanted, it was her own tears. She didn't know how to cry. Tears are worth more than blood. Why weren't you in the lodge?'

'I was. I couldn't intervene. We were all there, even the *camorrista* from last night. Questions of honour and respect have to be resolved on their own. No one else can intervene. You did the right thing, leaving the knife there.'

'It was you who taught me respect for the knife, that it has to be used to save someone, and isn't for anything else. So you were there watching.'

'Yes, and the first blood wasn't enough. The youth had let it be known that no one should intervene until the last blood. I knew you weren't going to die, but I didn't know how you'd manage. When I saw you circling the courtyard, I knew what you had in mind. You were looking for the heat in his face, the spot where he'd be dazzled. I'd never imagined you such an expert.'

'The sun was in my eyes as soon as I came into the courtyard. I thought I'd get him to that spot. Don Gaetano, I also knew I wasn't going to die. It was one of your thoughts. I heard it in my head. I'm beginning to hear thoughts myself.'

'I know. Yesterday you won at *scopa*. You're finished learning from me.'

The ships of the American Sixth Fleet, the aircraft carrier and its escort left the bay in formation. The light grey of their paint faded on the open sea. It was the colour of my ruined jacket. My light grey, too, was going off to sea. I'd have time to mend the cut in the sleeve and wash off the blood.

'Let me know about Anna, whether she's cured.'

We didn't say a single word about the young man who'd died. It was hopeless, considering where the knife had entered.

'Who knows where they're going,' I said in the direction of the warships.

'Not home. And nor are you. You're going over there.' He pointed to the south and to the west. I looked at the books and school notebooks on my knee. Goodbye to school. The lessons had all ended at once. I was losing the city that had taught me, losing Anna, Don Gaetano, Don Raimondo's books. *'T'aggia 'mpara' e t'aggia perdere.'* I have to teach you, and then I have to let you go. The city was pushing me out to sea. I couldn't continue with the life that had brought me up, ready like a calzone for the hot oil. It had turned me and then turned me over again, floured me and then thrown me into the iron skillet. In one of his poems, Salvatore Di Giacomo wishes to be a small fish caught in the beautiful hands of Donn'Amalia, who flours him and puts him into the pan. It was happening to me. Donn'Amalia was the city and the iron skillet the sea.

'Don Gaetano, being tired makes you think silly things.'

★

We ate at an *osteria* at the port. He gave me my ticket, documents, money. His savings.

'I'll return them to you. It won't be like the knife, which I'll repay by giving one to someone else. I'll bring this money back to you.'

I said the right things, rambling on. How did I know what I'd find in Argentina? How would I manage there? Don Gaetano presented me with a pack of Neapolitan playing cards and a Spanish grammar. We went to take a photo for the document. Don Gaetano went by a printer's to forge the stamp.

I embarked at sunset.

I saw the lights go on along the bay from Posillipo to Sorrento, so many white handkerchiefs waving goodbye to the open eyes of the departing. The people around me were drenched in tears. The people around me aren't in first class. They don't have return tickets.

I'm writing these pages now in a lined notebook while the ship heads towards the other end of the world. Around us the ocean moves, or lies still. They say that tonight we'll cross the Equator.

Born in Naples in 1950, Erri De Luca is one of Italy's bestselling novelists, whose work has been translated into many languages. He was awarded the France Culture Prize in 1994, the Fémina Etranger in 2002, and in 2013 he received the European Prize for Literature. He is also a translator from Ancient Hebrew and Yiddish. A passionate mountain climber, he currently lives in the countryside near Rome.

Jill Foulston is a writer and editor. Her other translations include novels by Piero Chiara and Augusto De Angelis.